Pork Pie Pandemonium

Albert Smith's Culinary Capers

Recipe 1

Steve Higgs

A Melton Mowbray Pork-pie
Strange pie that is almost a passion!
O passion immoral for pie!
Unknown are the ways that they
fashion
Unknown and unseen of the eye.
The pie that is marbled and mottled,
The pie that digests with a sigh:
For all is not Bass that is bottled,
And all is not pork that is pie.

- Richard Le Gallienne.

Table of Contents:

Extra Portion of Meat

The scream cut through the air at such a volume that Albert could have heard it if he was in the next county. By his side, his assistance dog, Rex Harrison, reacted, taking his eyes off the diced pork for the first time since they came in.

The screamer was a woman in her late twenties called Claire. Albert knew her name because everyone in the class had been given a large white sticker to write their names on. She was here with her boyfriend, a tall, skinny lad called Kevin who looked to be younger than her but not by much. Her eyes were as wide as any persons he had ever seen, and she was staring at the counter in front of her in an accusatory manner.

Then, she turned around and threw up.

Albert took that in his stride; he had never been affected by people vomiting. With his wife, he raised three children, and it had always been he that dealt with their sickness. She dealt with the poop.

As everyone else backed away, Albert found himself curious and walking around to Claire's side of the table before he thought about what he was doing. He didn't have to go far, his eyesight, providing he wasn't trying to look at something close up, was pretty good. Arriving on her side of the table, he spotted what had affected her so. There was a thumb resting on top of her pile of pork.

Teaching the class, where attendees got to raise their own handmade pork pie, was a short woman in her fifties called Belinda. 'It's someone's thumb,' she observed, rather unnecessarily, since everyone could already see it. Belinda wore a navy-blue apron on which the firm's logo and name were emblazoned. Agnew's Perfect Pork Pie Emporium stretched across her chest above a picture of a tasty looking pork pie. Like everyone else in

1

the room, her blond hair was encased in a net to stop hair falling into the food. The net struck Albert as a little unkind in his case since he only had about eighteen hairs left on his scalp and the whole concept of bothering with them was, quite frankly, ridiculous since they let him bring his German shepherd assistance dog, Rex Harrison, in with him. The dog wore a hair net on his head too, Albert's silent dig at the pointless adherence to rules. Rex didn't look happy about the net.

When Belinda moved in with a bowl, clearly intending to remove the thumb, he raised his voice, 'Don't touch that, please.'

Belinda's head snapped around along with everyone else's. Suddenly on the spot now that all eyes in the room were looking his way, Albert gave them his serious expression. 'I'm a retired detective superintendent from Kent. I'm afraid we need to treat this as a crime scene and bring in the local police.'

'But I have another class in an hour,' Belinda protested.

Pursing his lips and shrugging, Albert said, 'I'm afraid that is unlikely to proceed. Do you want to call the police yourself?'

A teenage girl burst into the room, flinging the door open in her haste. She looked to be sixteen or seventeen and was also wearing one of the firm's aprons. 'What was that scream?' she asked, concern etched on her face.

'You need a hair net to be in here,' snapped Belinda.

Albert expected the young woman to be cowed and apologise, but she narrowed her eyes instead. 'Oh, be quiet, Belinda. You have a dog in here for goodness sake.'

Rex Harrison sniffed the air, thinking to himself, not for the first time, that humans liked to mess around with their food before they ate it. He could never see the need for all the fuss. He licked his lips, there was a pile of pork just inches from his nose and no one was paying any attention to it.

'Don't even think about it,' said Albert, leaning down to make sure Rex Harrison knew the comment was aimed at him.

Rex thought something impolite in response and put his head down obediently. He didn't take his eyes off the pile of pork though.

The teenage girl could see the cluster of people forming a ring around the thumb so came into the room just as Albert spoke up. 'There's a human thumb in your meat mix. You need to call the police so they can identify who it belongs to. Is the meat brought in from somewhere?'

'Goodness, no!' exclaimed Belinda. 'It is all diced by hand on the premises.'

Kevin, the boyfriend of the young woman who found the thumb sniggered. 'Diced by hand. Nice one.'

The unnamed girl in the firm's livery was now staring at the thumb as it sat atop the small mound of meat at Claire's station. Albert wondered who she was since she was very young to be in a position of authority. She had brown hair pulled into a ponytail that hung down her back to a point between her shoulder blades. Her brown eyes were bright and lively, sitting above high cheekbones. She was an attractive young woman, Albert observed idly. She reminded him a bit of his Petunia when they first met. The girl was five feet eight inches tall and a hundred twenty pounds. Years of being a cop made the assessment of descriptive features second nature. While Albert noted what she looked like, she bit her lip as if trying to reach a decision. After a second or so she nodded her head before

3

turning back to Belinda at the head of the table. 'Belinda can you call the police, please?'

Belinda gave a frustrated sigh. 'Just pick it out, Donna. I've another class in an hour.'

Albert thought he might have to step in or call the police himself, but Donna wasn't to be swayed by her older co-worker. 'Now, please, Belinda.'

'You're not the boss here, Donna,' snapped Belinda, tearing at the bow to undo her apron. 'I'll not be given orders by a child. See how long you've got a job when your mum finds out her best cook walked out.' Then she threw her apron on the floor, followed it with the hairnet and stormed out. The door slammed behind her.

Donna made eye contact with the people around her, all of them paying customers. 'I'm very sorry, everyone. This class is over. If you come out to the front counter, I will give everyone a full refund and a coupon to rebook at half price.'

'But we are only visiting Melton Mowbray today,' complained a woman to her left. It prompted other complaints and Albert thought the poor girl was going to have a fight to get them to leave until another man spoke up. He was in his late sixties, grey hair going white above dark brown eyebrows and next to him, a woman of similar age standing close enough that they had to be husband and wife.

'It's not the poor girl's fault. There is a thumb in the meat. I for one do not wish to make a pork pie to take home that may have other parts of the same person in it.' He turned his attention to Donna. 'Thank you for the offer of a refund. Good luck with the police.' With that, he went to the door, the rest of the class following though many continued to mutter.

4

At the door, the woman who complained first nudged her husband. 'There's another place across the street. I bet they don't have thumbs in the meat. Let's go there. Look everyone, they have a class on at two o'clock.'

The door shut as the last person went out, leaving Donna in the room with Albert and Rex Harrison. The young woman reached into the back pocket of her jeans to produce a phone. 'I guess I'll call the police then,' she mumbled, still staring at the thumb.

'I'll do it,' volunteered Albert, reaching into his trouser pocket for his own phone and patting his other pockets to locate his reading glasses.

They're on your head, thought Rex Harrison, wondering how it was that the man misplaced them ten times a day.

Donna shook her head. 'No, it should be me. It's my family's shop.'

Smiling in a bid to help the woman relax, Albert dialled three nines anyway. 'It doesn't matter who calls them. The customers cannot leave though. They will need to give statements.'

Donna pulled a face, looking at the crowd waiting for their refunds. 'I don't think that is going to go down very well.' She heard his call connect as she opened the door to leave the classroom, the voice at the other end asked which service he required. She didn't want to deal with the restless customers, some of whom would be going straight across the road to the opposition, Simmons Perfect Pork Pie Palace, an outfit whose sole aim seemed to be to put her family's shop out of business. She didn't want to be in charge either, but mum had her appendix out in a rush yesterday which left her as the only Agnew standing. Like or not, it was her shop to run until her mum was well-enough to return to work.

Sabotage

The police were coming, which was duty done so far as Albert was concerned. He needed to hang around and give his statement, but he had nothing helpful to tell them. Outside the classroom, the small crowd were still bickering and moaning about not being given their refund, Donna using the tactic to keep them in place until the police arrived. Albert chose to stay where he was, spying a stool in the corner he could rest on. His knees were already beginning to ache.

Not getting to make and eat the porkpie was annoying, he had to admit. The pilgrimage to Melton Mowbray from his house in West Malling was the first leg of an intended tour of Britain. For fifty-two years his wife moaned at him for his inability to cook. It was good-natured mostly, she was happy to cook all the meals and he was only too happy to let her, but when she passed exactly twelve months ago yesterday, he had to fend for himself for the first time in his life. Born of that struggle came a bucket-list plan to learn to cook some of his favourite dishes. The British Isles had so many famous meals: Lancashire hotpot, Eton mess, Eccles cakes, Cumberland sausages, the list was long and extensive. For no better reason than he couldn't think of a reason why he shouldn't, he packed a small suitcase and a backpack and set off.

Three years ago, when aged seventy-five, he gave up driving. He no longer felt that his reactions and eyesight were sufficient to be behind the wheel, but rail, bus, and the power of his own two legs would get him to all the destinations he wanted to visit. People described him as sprightly now. It used to be strong or athletic, but those days were far behind him. His muscles were strong enough to support him but weak now by comparison with his glory days and hung from his frame in a disappointing way. At a shade over six feet he had been considered tall in his youth. Age had shrunk him so he stood just over five feet ten tall now, but while his body withered, and despite a spotty memory, he felt his mind was still sharp.

At his side was Rex Harrison, an assistance dog who was no such thing. Three years ago, his wife, Petunia, muttered and moaned about Albert needing an assistance dog because his hearing was going and because he was getting forgetful. He didn't think they would give him one and never bothered to apply to any of the charities who supply them because he expected the assessment process would be demeaning. However, he loved his wife and together they had enjoyed owning dogs in the past, so he cooked up a cunning plan. It required a little subterfuge, a purchase via an online shop, and a phone call to an old friend. It also relied on human nature to prevent people questioning what they were being presented with.

In retrospect, his plan hadn't been all that clever at all because he was stuck now with a large dog who was the only dog in the history of the Metropolitan police to have been fired for having a bad attitude. His phone call was to another retired cop who he knew to have children and grandchildren still serving. He could have called his own children, they were all police officers, but he didn't want them to know what he was up to. The call led to the team who trained the police dogs where, Albert assumed, he would be able to pick up a young dog who had failed the initial training. They tricked him though, seeing the chance to offload a dog who had been returned to them for rehoming just that week. Albert didn't find out about the attitude thing until weeks later when he questioned why his dog kept playing tricks on him. The purchase he made online was a harness and jacket with assistance dog down each side.

No one ever questioned it. Not once. And he got to take him everywhere, including into a pork pie making class which was his first attempt at learning to make a traditional British dish. His quest to become a capable cook was not going very well so far.

The jingle of a door opening heralded the arrival of two uniformed police officers. Agnew's shop was located at one end of Melton Mowbray's High Street and the cops were most likely on a routine patrol nearby which explained their fast response time.

Albert got up from his stool, his knees protesting with a click from each as he straightened. He was going to join the others outside now so the uniforms could do their job, but as he passed the thumb, still resting on top of the pile of glistening pork, he noticed something.

Leaning closer and pulling his reading glasses down off his head, he said, 'Here, Rex, what do you make of this?'

Albert made a habit of talking to the dog as if he expected a response, and it annoyed Rex that the human never listened to any of his replies. He moved in closer and jumped up to place his front paws on the table so he could get a better sniff.

Albert spotted a tattoo on the thumb, that was what drew his attention, but as he peered at it, he felt the familiar pull of a mystery. It was hardly the first time this had happened since he retired, his detective's brain refused to switch off. His children, and indeed his wife, accused him of meddling usually. Well, none of them were here now. He moved around to get a better look at the thumb from different angles.

The thumb was severed just behind the second knuckle, but it wasn't a clean cut. It looked a little mangled, as if it had been crushed and the skin was ragged as if torn. He needed to pick it up to get a better look but wouldn't allow his curiosity to overcome his desire to preserve the scene for the serving police officers. The tattoo was of a woman, though part of it was missing, still attached to the victim's hand. However, what he could

8

see had a lot of detail for such a small drawing, and though he had never been a fan of tattoos, he had to admire the skill involved. Around the woman's feet were small goldfish and she was posed as if treading water.

Rex sniffed deeply. He couldn't see the tattoo from his angle, but it wouldn't have meant anything to him if he could have. His nose was giving him all the information he needed. The severed digit stank of old engine oil and gasoline, two scents he associated with mechanics or places where mechanics worked on cars. Behind those smells he could detect the powder that came from WorkSafe gloves, a brand of glove favoured by mechanics.

'Can you step out there, please, sir?' The question wasn't really a question; it was a polite way for the police officer, now halfway through the door, to order Albert to remove himself. Albert knew the door had opened because the volume of chatter increased dramatically a moment before the cop spoke.

He straightened up, with a small groan as his back protested, and smiled at the young man in uniform. 'Yes, of course. Come along, Rex.'

Rex turned his head to look up at Albert, not that Albert was paying any attention. 'What about the meat?' he asked, his chuffing noise getting the fur on his head ruffled but no other kind of response.

In the shop's reception, just beyond the door, the customers were getting restless. They wanted their refund and they wanted to leave. The cop waiting for Albert to leave the classroom, gave up holding the door because he was getting accosted by a woman who insisted she be allowed to record her statement first because she had better things to do than stand around here all day. Her insistence led to an argument as other customers demanded the same.

9

No longer being observed, Albert quickly took out his phone and got a shot of the thumb, taking a few pics at different angles so he caught the tattoo in as much detail as possible. He had no particular reason to do so other than the familiarity of recording evidence. Knowing it was time to leave, he started toward the door. 'Come along, Rex. We really ought to go now.' Then he paused – Rex was suspiciously quiet. Narrowing his eyes to squint at the disobedient canine, Albert found Rex innocently looking back at him.

Rex tilted his head to ask, 'What?'

Not fooled for a moment, Albert looked at the table where one pile of porkpie filling was now missing, the spot where it ought to be, bearing a trace of moisture left over from the surface getting licked clean.

Albert just rolled his eyes. 'Come on, dog.'

Outside in the shop, things were calmer; the two uniformed officers managing to organise the crowd. As Albert joined them with Rex Harrison, the little bell above the door jingled again. Two detectives were coming in.

Albert knew they were detectives just by looking at them; he didn't need to see their ID. They got them out anyway, a man and a woman. The woman - the elder and more senior – spoke loud enough for everyone to hear. 'I am Detective Sergeant Moss. This is my colleague Detective Constable Wright.' She indicated the man to her left. 'The officers will record your name and address and take a telephone number where they can contact you. After that you will be free to go.'

DS Moss looked to be in her early forties. She wore a business suit that was a little crumpled and had seen better days. It was warm out today so perhaps she chose it because it was lightweight. She was quite short, maybe five feet and two inches, Albert estimated, and retained a trim figure that suggested plenty of exercise. Her partner, a younger man in his mid-twenties and Caribbean by racial origin, was much taller at six feet four inches and carrying a good deal of excess weight around his middle. He too wore a suit, but his was sharp and new by comparison.

Albert found a handy seat and used it to rest his legs. Rex placed his head on Albert's lap so he could stroke it and fuss the fur behind his ears. For Albert, it meant he had something to pretend to be focussed on while he eavesdropped on what Donna was telling DS Moss.

The two detectives were doing their job, yet in a bare-minimum way, it seemed to Albert. They were going through the steps with little interest. It was as if they'd been assigned a case to investigate but didn't see a crime.

'You say the meat is butchered on the premises?' DS Moss confirmed.

'That's right,' said Donna. 'We get a fresh delivery every day which is then prepared for use the next day. It is the same meat we use in the class as we use for the pies we sell.'

As the people from the class filed out of the shop, one or two at a time, a uniformed officer turned the sign around to show the world outside the shop was now closed. Donna saw him do it and sighed. It was her first full day in charge, and she felt like a failure already.

There were two women working the counter in the shop; Denise and Mandy, and two men who worked in the back called Jacob and Alan. The men prepared the meat and made the aspic. The ladies made the pastry, and all four hand-formed the pies each morning, starting at five o'clock so the pies were fresh on the shelf each day when the shop opened at nine.

DS Moss went through a dozen routine questions about whether there were other staff who worked at the shop and who else had access to the property? How many keys there were and who had them? Who delivered the meat? Donna answered them all one at a time. Albert learned that her mother owned the shop and was in hospital having her appendix removed. That was how a teenager came to be in charge today. When she talked about it, Albert watched the faces of the other staff. Denise was in her late sixties, he estimated, maybe even her early seventies. He wondered how she felt about a teenage girl running things when she must have so much more experience. Belinda made it clear she didn't accept Donna's rule, but how did the others feel? Did they see her as a child?

'Any idea how the thumb might have got into the meat?' DS Moss asked. 'If the meat is delivered the night before as whole cuts which are then hand butchered on site, how did a thumb get added to the mix?'

Donna pursed her lips as if trying to decide what to say. 'I think this is sabotage.'

Albert's head snapped around and up at her comment, surprised and intrigued by the statement.

'What makes you say that?' asked DS Moss.

Donna nodded with her head, a motion to draw their attention out of the large front window. 'Simmons Perfect Pork Pie Palace across the street are always playing dirty tricks on us. We are the established provider. Our pies win all the awards, but they have a small factory out the back which produces ten times as many pies as us each day. Their quality is terrible but they mass produce so their prices are lower and they keep targeting our big customers. Not everyone cares enough about taste.'

'Oh, I know,' gushed Detective Constable Wright. 'I eat your pies every week. They are just scrummy. I only ever tried a Simmons pie once.' He gave an exaggerated shudder at the memory.

Donna smiled at the compliment. 'I thought you looked familiar.'

'I come in every Saturday,' he beamed.

'Wright?' DS Moss cautioned him with a bored tone. His smile ran for cover as he folded his lips in to stop talking. 'Where was I?' DS Moss asked herself. 'Oh, yes; saboteurs. You think someone at a rival establishment might have placed a thumb in your meat in a bid to damage your business.' Moss said it as a statement but made it sound ridiculous, her voice dripping with incredulity.

'Um, maybe?' replied Donna, sounding far less sure now.

'The thumb hasn't been severed from its owner for long,' said Albert standing up.

DS Moss looked his way. 'We'll get to you in a moment, sir.'

She meant to dismiss him, but Albert kept right on talking, 'It means the owner is almost certainly in hospital right now, and if not, then ought to be showing up there really soon. It wasn't severed, you see? It appeared to have been ripped off.'

Now DS Moss looked more interested. 'Ripped off? Your name, please, sir?'

'Albert Smith. I'm a retired detective superintendent from Kent. I just happened to be taking the class today.'

'He stopped Belinda from throwing it in the bin. She wanted to get on with her class,' added Donna.

DS Moss nodded and started to move toward the classroom. Her whole attitude had changed in a heartbeat. What was a duff case with a misplaced thumb might now be a crime worthy of her attention. 'I think we should see this thumb.'

Refund

Albert decided to stick around; it wasn't as if he had anywhere else to be and the day was turning out to be more interesting than expected. His timely announcement about the thumb meant he was included now as they went back toward the classroom. They were interrupted before they could move very far by a man as he barged into the shop. On his shoulder was another man, this one wielding a camera and taking shot after shot of the surprised faces inside.

The first man held his phone in his right hand, clearly using it to record as he spoke. 'Famous pork pie shop selling pies filled with human parts, any comment?'

'What!' screeched Donna.

'Will you be renaming the shop? Sweeney Todd's Human Pie Emporium perhaps?'

Albert guessed that the man was a hack reporter, reacting quickly and trying to get the scoop on a local story, but quite willing to exaggerate to sensationalise it.

DS Moss gave him her bored face. 'Peterson, you really are a scumbag.'

Undeterred, he pushed the recording device her way. 'Police suppress truth yet again. Backhander bribes suspected as public health is put at risk.'

'You print whatever garbage headline you like, Peterson,' she snapped, jabbing her finger at the two uniforms who she felt should have been preventing entry.

Getting no joy from her, Peterson swung his device under Donna's nose. Standing in the customer part of the shop, where the rest of the staff were still behind the counter, she was an easy target to pick out. The uniformed cops were hustling both him and his photographer back toward the door, but not fast enough to stop him hassling her some more.

'Will you be publishing the new recipe? Where do you get your human parts from?' then he swung it back toward DS Moss, 'Is this part of our justice system? Are the police working with Agnew's Pork Pie Emporium to get rid of local criminals by eating them?'

As his shoulder hit the doorframe, his phone got knocked from his hand to skitter across the floor. The uniformed officers had their hands out to their sides to walk him from the shop, but he tried to duck under them now to retrieve his phone.

Unfortunately for Peterson, it landed next to Rex's feet, and before Albert could consider stopping him, the dog picked it and bit it. A very definite crunching sound came from the dog's mouth – not the sound one would wish to hear from a piece of delicate electronic equipment.

'Spit it out, Rex,' Albert instructed.

Rex was happy to do so. He thought the man had thrown it to him and perhaps it was a chew toy since it didn't smell like food. It wasn't nice in his mouth though. It didn't squeak amusingly and didn't seem like something he could chase. Into Albert's hand went the pieces of phone and a good deal of slobbery spit.

With a smile, because he wasn't a fan of reporters, Albert said, 'Here you are,' as he tipped the fragments into Peterson's disappointed hands. Then the cops backed him out of the door and closed it.

DS Moss jabbed a finger at them. 'You, stand guard outside. You, lock the door.' Now that no one else was getting in, she turned back toward the classroom door, and muttering, went inside.

The thumb was exactly where it had been, exactly where Claire found it forty minutes ago. It sat right on top of the pile of meat as if it has been positioned there deliberately, or perhaps … fell there, I thought, looking up. Above the thumb was nothing but solid ceiling.

'Who places the meat out for the customers?' asked DS Moss.

'The instructor,' Donna replied. 'For this class, it would have been Belinda.'

Moss said, 'I shall need contact details for her,' but she didn't look up. She was bent over to inspect the thumb, much as Albert had been earlier.

Rex sniffed the air again. He could still smell the mix of old engine oil and gasoline. He could also detect a scent of it on the air that wasn't coming from this room. There was a mechanic's place nearby somewhere. That is where they ought to be looking. Content they would work it out sooner or later, he laid down for a rest.

'Ma'am, there's something here,' Wright said excitedly. 'One of the piles of meat has been taken. I think that might be significant.'

'My dog ate it,' admitted Albert, stopping the young detective before he could jump to a wild conclusion.

Folding his lips in again, Wright walked around to join DS Moss near the thumb. She straightened up and exhaled through her nose in a slow, deliberate manner. 'Okay. I'm calling this a crime scene.' She looked directly at Albert. 'I'm afraid I am going to have to ask you to leave. Wright will take your details but retired superintendent or otherwise, I

17

need to shut this place off and get the crime scene guys in. Thank you for your help.'

Albert was surprised to have been allowed to stay here this long. It had been fun, a blast from the past in some ways to be at the pointy end where a case is just being started. Young Donna was looking more than a little lost, but it wasn't for him to console her. The shop would be shut down, the paper Peterson worked for would probably print something horrible, but the shop had been around long enough, and he felt sure it would reopen soon once the matter was cleared up.

He waved the girl goodbye as he left her to deal with the police and went merrily on his way.

Outside the shop, Albert paused to decide what to do with the rest of his day. He came here only to make a pork pie but didn't fancy going to the other shop. He could see people in there now - some of them from the abandoned class. He had eaten Agnew's pork pies in the past and considered them to be the gold standard. If he couldn't make one now, he could always push on to Bakewell and circle back here at the end of his trip.

'Where shall we go, Rex?' he asked the dog.

Rex swung his head around to look up at the human. He could smell the garage. 'I think we should go this way,' he said with his eyes. 'Around the corner is where that thumb was before it ended up in the tasty meat shop.'

Albert looked down at the dog. 'I swear it looks like you are trying to tell me things sometimes. Let's go for some lunch, shall we? Maybe I shall have a half pint of stout and some fish and chips. Would you like a glass of stout? Would you, boy?'

Rex wanted to roll his eyes at the easily distracted human. 'There's a crime to solve, you know?' he indicated, knowing it was hopeless to expect the human to understand. A glass of stout sounded good, though, so he started walking, the human seeming to know where he was going even though Rex knew how badly his nose worked.

Many hours after lunch, and back at his B&B, Albert was surprised to have his quiet afternoon of reading disturbed by the landlady. His timetable, having arranged his tour of Britain with the help of his daughter, Selina, and granddaughter, Apple-Blossom, was to take a train to Bakewell tomorrow. It meant he had time to kill this afternoon so had chosen to relax in the rather nice garden the landlady kept behind her house. It even had a small river babbling along beside it as a delightful countryside touch.

'You have a visitor,' Mrs Worsley announced. 'It's a young lady,' she added as if that ought to mean something.

Albert was dumbfounded, but he thanked Mrs Worsley, closed his book with a prayer that he would remember the page even though he couldn't remember to pick up a bookmark, and shuffled out to the front door to see who it was with Rex Harrison trailing behind him. This was his first visit to Melton Mowbray which made him question who on Earth could be calling. The answer, once he got to the door, was obvious.

'Oh, hello, Donna. What brings you here?'

The teenage girl from the pork pie shop had an envelope in her right hand. 'You left so quickly, I never got to give you your refund. You were really helpful this morning so I thought I would drop it off in person.' Her apron was gone, replaced by a bright red puffy jacket that zipped up the middle to ward off the cool Autumn air. It matched the bright red Nike running shoes on her feet. Her legs were shod in tight, bleached, skinny jeans which just looked uncomfortable to wear in Albert's opinion. He felt fashion died when people stopped wearing flared jeans.

'How did you know where to find me?' Albert asked, his forehead crinkling in confusion.

'It was on the waiver you filled in.'

'Oh, yes.' His memory really was getting spotty these days. Donna was holding the envelope up for him to take. Albert wasn't worried about the money, it seemed harsh for the firm to have to hand it all back. 'Do you think you will be closed for long?' he asked.

Donna cast her eyes down and when she looked back up, she had a tear leaking from her left eye. Albert immediately reached for his handkerchief, mumbling an apology.

'That reporter had a story about us on his paper's website within the hour. He didn't even bother to find out any facts,' Donna said as she accepted the handkerchief in exchange for the envelope. 'The health ministry will have to recertify the shop if the police forensics people find any human flesh on the premises. They are there now inspecting it all. They took away all our produce and all the meat for tomorrow's batch, not that we will be open tomorrow. There's been a rush of cancellations already, so even if we did reopen tomorrow, the classes will be half empty. It's going to take ages to undo this damage. Mum is terrified because we don't have enough cashflow to pay everyone back. If any more people cancel, we might be in real trouble.' The young woman's face was turning to a tear-filled mess which left Albert wondering what the right thing to do might be.

Rex Harrison didn't understand crying, but he recognised when a human was upset and knew that getting attention from him was wonderful enough to cheer anyone up. Sitting by his human's feet, he leaned forward to nudge the young female human's hand.

She sniffed and wiped at her tears, then reached down to ruffle his fur. 'What's his name?' she asked.

'It's Rex Harrison,' Albert told her.

She wrinkled her eyebrows. 'That's an unusual name.'

Albert explained, 'He was a police dog before he switched careers to be an assistance dog. They get hundreds of new dogs every year and struggle to come up with names, so they pick a theme. He was taken in when they were in Hollywood month.'

'There's an actor called Rex Harrison?' Donna had clearly never heard of him, but had her phone out, like all kids seem to do now. Moments later she had a list of his films and a picture of him on her screen. 'Dr Doolittle. I've heard of him.'

To change the subject, and because he was curious, he asked, 'You told the detectives earlier that you thought the chaps in the rival pork pie place might be behind it. Why is that?'

Donna patted Rex on his head again and handed back Albert's handkerchief. 'They have been quite vocal about wanting our business. Mum says there's enough customers for us to both exist without anyone feeling the pinch, but they have tried all kinds of dirty tricks. They tried to bribe our staff into giving away our recipe. They shut off our electricity and slashed the tyres on our delivery van. They came into our shop and *accidentally* dropped a bucket of dye into our pastry.'

'I see. Getting hold of a fresh thumb seems like quite an escalation,' Albert observed. 'That's not something you can just decide to do. Could it have come in with the meat?'

Donna shrugged. 'I guess I don't know where it came from, but it might shut us down regardless of its origin.'

'What if we found the owner?' Albert asked, surprising himself because he hadn't planned to volunteer his services. Too late now, the offer had been made.

Donna searched his face, staring up at him with caramel coloured eyes. 'You mean like solve the crime ourselves?' The hope in her voice almost broke Albert's heart. He couldn't change his mind now. 'I remember now. You told the police you were a retired supervisor or something.'

'Um, yes. A retired detective superintendent. It was a while ago, mind you.'

Donna's imagination was off and running already. 'We could find out how they did it. Get all the evidence and then nail those Simmons brothers to the wall. Yeah!' She punched her left fist into her right palm. 'I bet they killed someone and cut his thumb off just so they could put it in my mum's shop.' Then she gasped. 'I bet one of the customers was a plant. Maybe it was the woman who found it. She could have placed the thumb there and then screamed and pretended like it was there the whole time.'

'Maybe,' Albert admitted. He had heard worse theories though he thought the rival bakers murdering people seemed unlikely.

Vibrating with excitement, Donna asked, 'How do we get started?'

Rex was happy to be out for a walk. It was somewhere completely new, and the air was filled with lots of unusual and unexpected smells. There was an abandoned kebab ahead. It was in the road, but it couldn't be more than a couple of days old. The scent coming from it was a kaleidoscope to his nose, but then he caught the familiar smell of a squirrel.

Albert saw Rex's head come up, his ears pricking as the dog momentarily froze. 'Uh-oh.' He'd seen this before and recognised it from previous dogs too.

'What's up?' asked Donna, seeing the old man begin to crouch as if getting into a brace position.

Albert didn't get time to answer as a squirrel darted out from a bush twenty yards ahead and Rex attempted to fly.

'No, Rex!'

Rex didn't even hear his human shouting. Every fibre of his being had been trained upon the road ahead because he knew there was a squirrel here somewhere. Then it popped out of the undergrowth to snag a nut and instinct took over. He had to get it, he had to stop it taunting him with its skippety little hops. Squirrels had to die. He didn't know why, but his legs were moving before his brain told them to.

Four bounds later, he reached the end of his lead and almost snapped his neck.

Albert saw him go, shouted at the top of his lungs, even though he knew it would make no difference, and prepared for the jolt he knew was coming. Mercifully, they were next to a road that had railings to separate the people from the cars. He quickly looped the lead around a bar and held on.

Rex picked himself up, glared grumpily at the human who was shouting something again and looked at the spot the squirrel occupied a moment before. He could have caught that one. He really could have. The fact that he had never caught one before meant the law of averages had to be on his side. The human was tugging for him to come back, so he sat down and refused to move. When the human tugged a little harder, he folded out his legs and laid himself flat. 'Try moving me now,' he thought.

Albert gave up, accepting the inevitable as he went to the dog since the dog clearly wasn't coming to him. The girl couldn't stop laughing.

'That was so funny,' she giggled. 'He sure is a headstrong dog.'

Albert didn't think it was all that funny; his shoulder hurt from getting tugged so hard. 'You said the tattoo parlour wasn't far away?' he asked to move past the subject of his dog's attitude.

Donna pointed ahead. 'It's just around the corner.' They chose to walk into the town centre. It wasn't far from where he was staying, his choice of B&B quite deliberate for its geography. There were lots of bars and restaurants around, but they walked by all of them. They were looking for tattoo parlours. Truthfully, Albert thought this was a silliness. They weren't going to solve a crime like some clever duo in a mystery book. He indulged her because he had nothing much better to do and he had kind of walked himself over his own trapdoor.

Donna was too young to have her own ink but said she wanted tattoos and had designs already picked out. Her mum didn't approve; neither did Albert for that matter but he kept quiet. Some of her friends had them and she always went along if she could. She hadn't noticed the tattoo on the severed thumb, but seeing a picture, she claimed it could only be the work of one or possibly two people in the town. No one else was good enough for such finely detailed work in her opinion. It gave them a starting point, so here they were on their way to visit the first shop.

Albert didn't have any tattoos. He didn't have any piercings either. They just weren't his thing, though he dabbled with the idea of an earring for a while in the seventies because everyone else was getting them. His career in the police saw him visit plenty of tattoo parlours and they all looked the same to his mind – seedy little places on back streets where the rent was low.

To his surprise, the first place was right in the middle of the town centre and it was plush inside like a high-end salon. A young woman sat behind a glossy enamel reception desk. It was bright white and underlit with softly glowing pink neon.

'Good evening, welcome to Great Inkspectations. Are you looking for anything in particular today?' The young woman had six or seven piercings in her left ear and one of those big earlobe stretchy things he could never remember the name for. Her right ear was devoid of any jewellery. She also had steelwork in her nose, her lips, her eyebrow and in the centre of both cheeks. Her natural hair colour was long gone, replaced by jet black and fire engine red, and her outfit was torn and mangled as if her walk to work involved a bear encounter.

Donna said, 'Hey, sick threads.'

The receptionist smiled. 'Thank you.'

Unsure what he was supposed to say, Albert copied Donna, 'Um yes, very sick.' Then to himself, he mumbled, 'Like someone threw up.'

'I'm sorry?' the young woman asked, one eyebrow raised and her smile no longer in place.

'Nothing,' Albert lied. 'Got a bit of a cough. I was hoping to ask a question, actually,' he moved quickly on. Taking his phone from his pocket, he planned to show the receptionist the tattoo on the thumb.

Donna got in ahead of him. 'Is Grunge in tonight, Kerry? I have a tattoo to show him. I'm trying to find out if it is his work or not.'

The young woman hadn't introduced herself, which Albert didn't like. He felt people in customer facing roles should do so, or wear a name badge, but then he saw that Donna knew the woman's name because it was tattooed across her neck in large letters.

'Sure, he's in,' Kerry replied. 'He's got a customer with him right now. You want to wait?'

The wait wasn't very long, thankfully, a gentleman called Grunge, of all things, appeared from behind a frosted door no more than ten minutes later. He was extremely inked, complex interwoven designs disappearing up his sleeves from his wrists and down his top from his neck. He wore a nice suit and an oxford shirt with a button-down collar. He had no tie, but his chosen outfit, complete with polished brogues, seemed incongruous against his skin art and in this setting. His outfit made Albert feel underdressed. He chose loose slacks and tennis shoes because they were the most comfortable on his bunions plus a cotton shirt and windbreaker on top.

Donna stood up to greet him and he recognised her instantly. 'Hi, Donna,' he gave her a cursory hug. 'By yourself tonight? You know I can't ink you until you are eighteen without a parent present. Are you here to discuss designs, because I'm kind of busy?' He was pushing her away but being nice about it; a sensible ploy if he knew she wanted to spend her money once old enough.

'Actually, I have a question,' she replied. 'It's to do with a tattoo.'

'Well, you came to the right place.' He smiled like a game show host. Then he seemed to notice Albert and Rex Harrison for the first time. Albert chose to hang back a few feet while his young friend spoke, but now Grunge's attention swung his way, he extended his hand.

'Albert Smith. I'm helping this young lady investigate a crime and hoped you might help us identify a tattoo.'

'Investigate?' Grunge's voice rose an octave. 'Like you're some kind of private eye or something? Aren't you a little old for that?'

Albert was surprised by the young man's directness. It was rude but he didn't react. Instead, he smiled and flipped his eyebrows. 'I am too old, yes. Nevertheless, I hope you can assist us.' He fished his phone from the inside left pocket of his windbreaker.

'It's really intricate work,' said Donna. 'That's why I thought of you.' She was buttering him up.

Grunge took the offered phone. 'Ewww, dude! Is that someone's thumb?'

Donna grabbed his arm, leaning in close to whisper. 'Be cool, man. Do you recognise the ink? Is it your work?'

Grunge fixed his face, forcing his upturned lip back into place as he focussed on looking at the artwork and not the denuded bone poking out from the ruined flesh. After a few seconds, he shook his head. 'That's not one of mine.' He looked up. 'It's good, don't get me wrong. I would be proud to have done the work, but I cannot claim it.'

'Any idea whose work it might be?' Albert asked.

'This is serious ink,' Grunge replied.

'Boris?' asked Donna.

Grunge nodded. 'He's the only one for miles that could attempt this. There are others in the country, of course, but if this was done locally. It would have to be Boris.'

Albert said, 'Boris?'

Twenty minutes later they were in Inktasia, a more back-alley operation; the kind Albert was used to.

Boris was Russian, a heritage he held onto, but his accent bore no trace of his motherland. It made Albert wonder how many generations removed he might be, though he didn't ask. There wasn't time to because their second visit was a hit.

'Yeah, that's one of mine,' Boris proudly admitted less than a second after they showed him the picture. 'Fella came in wanting something original. He had a sketch of what he wanted even.'

'Do you keep records,' Albert asked.

Boris raised an eyebrow. 'Of course.'

Albert knew it wasn't a requirement to keep records of who had what tattooed and when, but it was common practice. Behind him on the floor, Rex Harrison stretched out. He didn't like this place. It smelled of blood. The humans appeared to be trying to work out who the thumb belonged to but, as usual, they were going about it all the wrong way.

Over at the counter, Boris paused. 'Have you got a warrant or something?'

Donna glanced at Albert who just smiled. 'Why would we need a warrant? This is just a friendly question. A man left his thumb behind and we are trying to find out who the man is, that's all.'

The tattoo artist seemed to debate what he wanted to do for a few moments, but reached a decision, possibly that this was the quickest way to get rid of the old man, and tapped his computer mouse into life.

Donna and Albert waited patiently while Boris leaned over the top of the chair to use the computer rather than taking a seat. It didn't take long to find what he wanted. 'Fella's name is Mark Whitehouse.'

Albert didn't want to trust his memory. 'Do you have a piece of paper I could write that on by any chance?'

'It's okay, I've got it,' Donna said quickly as her thumbs danced across the screen of her phone.

'An address?' Albert asked hopefully.

Boris straightened up from being bent over the back of the chair. 'No. I wouldn't give out a customer's address even if I did have it.' His eyes were narrowed at the odd couple now. They were asking too many questions for his liking. He remembered the customer as a dodgy, criminal sort. The kind that thinks he's a bit of a wide boy and likes to play up the persona. 'What do you plan to do with this man if you find him? I don't want him to know that you got his name from me, okay.'

Donna blurted, 'Of course, not. Nothing will come back to you.'

However, Boris's reaction tweaked Albert's curiosity. 'Why is that important to you?' he asked.

Now Boris felt a little stuck. He didn't want to sound scared, not in front of the girl, but the truth was that he didn't want the man coming back here. He was one of those customers that you hope you never see again.

In the end, he decided he would rather look weak. 'He had a dangerous edge.'

'Can you describe him?'

At Albert's question, an image swam into Boris's brain. 'He wasn't tall, maybe five feet seven inches, but he was broad and solidly built. Not like a bodybuilder but like a person who does manual labour all day every day and just builds up slabby blocks of muscle over time. His head was shaved down to nothing, but he had stubble on his face the day he came in here. It was trimmed across his cheeks and around his neck, so I think he keeps it that way.' Boris went on to tell them what he was wearing and about some of his other tattoos, none of which Boris had done and looked like amateur prison ink in his opinion.

Once he started talking, Albert and Donna got more than they bargained for, but Boris ran out of steam after a few minutes and they had all they needed: a name for the owner of the thumb.

Back outside the shop, Donna asked, 'What do we do now?'

Albert supressed a yawn. 'Now we leave it until tomorrow morning. I, for one, am tired, my dear. We have a name and that's enough to get us started. My son is still serving in the police down in Kent. I'll ask him to look up Mark Whitehouse. If he has a record, I should have an address for him in the morning. If he doesn't have a record, it may take a little longer but from Boris's description, I think we will know by breakfast.'

Donna was impressed. 'What about the Simmons brothers? Do you think we will be able to tie it to them?' she asked hopefully.

She was jumping the gun a bit, her desire to prove the firm across the road were behind her current business problems leading her in a direction that may yet prove erroneous. However, Albert thought it might be fun to explore the possibility. 'If you want to do some snooping, perhaps we should pay a visit to their shop tomorrow.'

'Ooh!' said Donna excitedly. 'How about if we take a class? They run them every day, mostly with drop-ins. They don't get the same level of bookings as mum because they are not the famous name in Melton Mowbray.'

Her idea had merit and appeal. 'Okay, Donna,' Albert smiled. 'I'll meet you tomorrow morning. What time is their first class?'

'It's eleven thirty. The sneaky gits time all their classes to start half an hour before ours,' she grumbled.

'Then I shall see you at eleven.'

They needed to go in different directions, Donna still lived with her mum on the other side of town from where they were. Albert felt he should offer to walk her safely home, Rex's surly nature ensured no one ever approached, but she declined his offer.

'It's not far,' she assured him.

He bade her goodnight and started back toward his B&B. 'Come along, Rex. I'd like a Horlicks before bed and if I have one too late, I'll be up peeing all night.' Albert tugged the lead.

'What are you up to, dad?' His son's question was not unexpected.

'Just helping someone,' Albert answered as honestly as he could without revealing that he had taken to snooping. Gary, Albert's eldest, was fifty-four years old and a detective superintendent in the Kent police just like his father had been. Albert had hoped his son would progress higher up the ranks, but Gary appeared quite content with his lot. He would retire next year with a fat pension, just as Albert had, and maybe then he would understand how retirement could get a little boring. Poking his nose in occasionally kept his mind sharp.

'It sounds like you are poking your nose in where it isn't wanted, dad,' Gary replied. 'Am I going to have to come up there and get you out of trouble?'

Albert frowned. 'I'm not doing anything that is going to get me into trouble, thank you, Gary. I am just looking into something. A young lady needed my help.'

'Dad, you sent me a name and asked me to find his address. He's a known criminal, dad. His file is an inch thick.'

'I thought they were all electronic files now,' Albert retorted quickly.

'You know what I mean, dad. I'm sending you an email now. Just don't go getting into trouble.' His son ended the call just as Albert's phone pinged with the incoming email. He had to press a few buttons to get to the right bit to read it and then search for his reading glasses again. Gary hadn't wanted Albert to take this trip. He didn't say it, but Albert knew his eldest son thought he was too old to be gallivanting around the countryside. 'What if you have a fall?' he has asked. 'What if you get confused?'

Albert wasn't senile yet, thank you.

The email contained a picture of Mark Whitehouse so now he knew what the man looked like. He had the kind of head one might described as bullet-like. It was shaved in the picture as Boris said it was, and his stubble was neatly trimmed. He wasn't very nice to look at; it was hard to imagine him smiling, and he did give off the dangerous vibe Boris mentioned. Albert met all kinds of people as a police officer and Mark Whitehouse looked like the kind of person who would pull a knife because someone looked at him in a way he didn't like.

Rex rolled over onto his paws, stretching out his back, shoulders, hips and then all the bits in between as he got ready to leave the B&B. He could tell his human was gearing up to go out; he had little routines. Right now, he was taking a fresh handkerchief to place in his right-hand trouser pocket. It went in with the loose coins to stop them rattling too much. Then he would pat his pockets to make sure he had everything, a sure sign that he wanted to go somewhere.

'Come on, Rex. Let's take a walk.'

Rex was always happy to go out. He didn't need the exercise but there was little fun in sleeping all day. The human took him out first thing each morning, walking down to the local park with him at home. This morning they had wandered around a bit until they found a park. Then, off the lead, Rex chased pigeons and sniffed where rabbits had been and did his best to mark every tree.

Albert bumped into Mrs Worsley near the door. 'I shall need to settle up for the extra days,' he said.

'Oh, there's no rush, dear. How long do you think you will stay?'

'Just an extra day or so, if that's alright?'

'No problem at all, dear. We are always quite quiet at this time of the year. You stay as long as you want.' Mrs Worsley bustled off down the hallway back toward the kitchen where the smell of bacon still hung in the air from breakfast. He patted his stomach at the memory. To Albert it seemed a universal truth that a decent full English could never be recreated at home and this morning's had been a corker.

He let himself out, heading back to the town centre and the pork pie shops as he thought about how long he might now stay. The Bakewell trip could wait a day or so; he certainly felt no need to rush at his time of life and sticking rigidly to a timetable was for fools – he had a crime to investigate.

It bothered him a little that he wasn't sure what the crime was.

A thumb is not a crime. However, tearing it off someone is, the presence of the thumb without the owner very much suggesting Mark Whitehouse might have come to a sticky end.

Arriving back at Agnew's Perfect Pork Pie Emporium, Albert expected to find Donna waiting. When he couldn't see her anywhere, he checked his watch to make sure he hadn't misread it earlier. It was almost ten past eleven, very much time to be getting into the shop across the street. Simmons Perfect Pork Pie Palace was open for business, a queue of people inside all buying their goods and yet more people forming a blob at one end of the counter away from the food. Albert assumed that was the class getting ready to go in but if Donna had changed her mind, did he bother to attend?

Rex was looking at Donna and wondering why his human was ignoring her. She was waiting outside the place they were in yesterday with all the meat. All the meat and the thumb that someone lost.

Albert looked around again, checking to see if Donna might be coming down the road. There were people going about their business, walking back and forth with bags or holding hands as couples do. Outside Donna's shop was a scruffy-looking young man. He had big work boots on and none of his clothes seemed to fit him very well. It was probably a new fashion Albert just didn't understand. When he glanced at him for the second time, because the young man was staring directly at him, the young man broke into a wide grin and started towards him. Was this going to be trouble? Rex Harrison would have something to say if the boy was aggressive.

'You didn't recognise me at all, did you?' said Donna.

Albert's eyebrows reached for the sky. It wasn't a young man at all. It was Donna in disguise. She had a wig over her long hair and a wispy beard like a young man might grow, plus she was wearing glasses. Now that he looked for it, he could see the swell of her breasts, but he would never have questioned her gender if she hadn't spoken.

'I have a friend who works as a movie makeup artist,' she explained, seeing the expression on Albert's face. 'The Simmons brothers know me. If I go in there to attend a class, they will kick me out.'

Ah, thought Albert, realising the purpose behind the disguise. 'Shall we say I am your grandfather?' he smiled, thinking the disguise was clever.

'Sure. Why not? Let's just hope that awful Toby Simmons isn't there today.'

'Is he one of the brothers?' Albert enquired as they neared the door.

'The son of the elder brother. He and I dated for a while. He might recognise me even with the disguise.'

35

Inside the shop was a press of people. They were all buying pork pies of varying flavours, plus other pies and pastries, bread, sausages and tracklements to go with them. Behind the counter were three men. They were good looking, broad shouldered, and very clearly all related. Two were brothers. The third man was at least twenty years younger and in his late teens. From the way Donna tensed up, Albert guessed he was Toby.

They were in fine mood and chatting loudly with their customers. 'Yes, well, we haven't concerned ourselves with what the competition are doing,' said one brother.

'No. We focus on making a superior product,' added the other, taking a twenty-pound note and handing over a bag filled with goodies. 'That was the right thing for us to do for our customers. Quality will always win.'

Then Toby spoke. 'Of course, we had no idea they were using human parts to fill their pork pies. It makes you wonder how long it had been going on and where they were getting the bodies from.'

Donna took a step forward, Albert's hand on her arm only just stopping her before she made a scene.

At the far-right end of the counter, the gaggle of people Albert noticed earlier were being addressed by a woman. 'How many have I got?' she stood on her tiptoes to see over their heads as she counted. 'Oh, perfect. Just the right number. It is you two as well, yes?' she asked Donna and Albert.

'That's Toby's mum, Lisa,' whispered Donna.

Albert nodded his understanding as the class began to file through a door ahead of them. He hadn't asked anyone about Rex Harrison yet; there hadn't been a chance. Rex wore his assistance dog vest and harness, but Albert still felt there was a need to announce the dog's presence.

Lisa Simmons was too busy taking charge and issuing instructions. Albert raised his hand but got ignored, plus he felt silly holding his hand up like a child, so he put it down again and tucked his dog beneath the table.

On the table was a sticker to write their names on much like yesterday in Agnew's class. Albert started patting his pockets; his reading glasses were here somewhere.

'I've got it,' said Donna in a deep voice. She didn't sound like a man. Rather, she sounded like a woman doing a very bad impression of a man. She finished her sticker and slapped it onto her shirt and then wrote his.

'That's an unusual name for a guy,' Toby's mum observed. 'I've never met a man called Donna before.'

Donna blushed, realising her mistake. 'Um, it's short for … Donnameche,' she blurted.

Across the room from them, which was a large oblong with a big stainless-steel table in the middle, a middle-aged man screwed up his face. 'Don Ameche? The B movie actor? Your mother named you after him?'

'Um, yeah?' said Donna carefully, then whispered from the side of her mouth, 'Who the heck is Don Ameche?'

Albert hoped they could get on with the class soon before any more attention swung their way. Donna's beard was beginning to peel away by her left ear. She was nervous and sweating enough to lift the glue.

At the head of the table, Toby's mum clapped her hands together to get the class's attention. 'Right everybody. Welcome to Simmons Perfect Pork Pie Palace, not to be confused with the lesser establishment across the street with a similar name. Today you will be making a hand raised pork pie ...'

'Why is it a lesser establishment?' asked Donna, interrupting the woman in full flow.

'Excuse me?'

'Not the right time for this,' whispered Albert.

Donna ignored him, unable to keep her anger in check. 'I'm just curious. You called it a lesser establishment, but they have been open for more than a century. It says so right across the street on their window.' All heads in the class turned to look across the street. 'Their pies have won awards. What is it that makes them a lesser establishment?'

'They don't appear to be open,' said the man who asked about Don Ameche.

'No,' Toby's mum smiled. 'They make inferior quality pork pies and finally got caught out yesterday when someone's thumb was found in the meat.'

'How do you know that's what happened?' asked Donna.

Albert thought his young friend was going to explode when Toby's mum questioned the quality of her mum's products, but Donna had been carefully goading the other woman into revealing her involvement.

It didn't work out that way. The man who kept speaking said, 'It's all over the news, mate. Everyone knows about it.'

Toby's mum tried to steer them back onto the subject of the class. 'Right, then, shall we get on with making our pastry? Now, does anyone know what type of pastry is used for a traditional pork pie?'

The class settled down and got underway which was a shame so far as Rex was concerned because he had been about to snag a piece of meat. It was just sitting there inches away from his nose. It smelled succulent and fresh. Just a few pieces, that couldn't hurt, surely.

Too late now, his human spotted what he was looking at and moved it out of the way. 'I think I'll just shift that back a bit. We wouldn't want it to go on the floor, now would we, Rex?'

'Speak for yourself,' replied Rex with a sigh.

Ten minutes later, the students were all beginning to fill their hand-formed pies with the provided handful of meat. Each pie was big enough to fill an open palm, and despite Donna's instance that her pies were better, Albert intended to eat his once it went through the oven – he'd been in Melton Mowbray for two days now and hadn't eaten so much as a crumb of pork pie yet.

Donna continued to mutter, but once the pies went in the oven, Albert knew they were going to get a chance to snoop. While their pies cooked, the students were treated to a tour of the pie factory at the back of the shop where Toby's mum would take them through all the stages of making what she insisted was Melton Mowbray's best pork pie.

As Lisa led them through a door at the other end of the room, Albert picked up Rex's lead. 'Come on, boy.' Albert wasn't sure how they would feel about Rex being in the factory, however, since no one had said anything yet, he decided to just take him along anyway.

Simmons factory wasn't a large place – forty yards by twenty perhaps - but it was stuffed with industrial equipment to shift the food from one end to the other with the minimal amount of human involvement.

'It's all done by machines,' Donna observed with horror. 'No wonder their meat looks so torn up; it gets minced by a robot. Ours is all cut by hand to keep the size even. It then gets mixed by hand to make sure the blend of shoulder, leg, belly and other cuts is the same in every pie.'

Albert didn't know how much difference that would make, but he wasn't going to question what Donna claimed. He'd never eaten one of this establishment's pork pies but was curious enough now to do a taste test if he ever got the chance.

'This is the meat mincer and mixer,' Lisa Simmons proudly told her audience. She'd led them into an open area between machines where a confluence of walkways met. The meat mixer was a large stainless-steel object, with a conveyer belt leading up to it. 'The meat is delivered ready-boned for efficiency and placed on the belt to lift it to the mincer/mixer. This is how Simmons' pies achieve such an even blend of meat. I'm going to lead you up on the raised walkway now so you can see into the machine. Please take care and do not touch anything.'

The group had to climb three steps to get up to the top of the mixer/mincer to then look down into it. Inside, steel teeth rotated about several spindles to turn whole cuts into tiny shreds of meat in seconds. Albert shuddered as a whole leg of pork dropped off the conveyor and vanished a moment later. The group filed down again where Lisa waited to lead them to see another process.

Being led up a long walkway between machines that towered over them, Albert snagged Donna's arm. They passed an unoccupied office. 'Let's look in here.'

Rex paused outside the office, sniffing the air. There was something familiar here, something barely detectible. He remembered the smell from his training, but no sooner did he pick up the scent than he lost it.

There was so much meat smell clogging his brain. The pies were all formed on the line and then taken through an oven on a conveyer belt. From there, the process finally needed a human to offload them onto cooling racks, but the whole factory stunk of freshly baked pork pie and Rex's chops were drooling.

His human gave his lead a tug, wanting him to move, but he held firm for a second as he tried to capture the smell again. He almost got it, but it was faint, and it kept eluding him. He knew the scent but couldn't get enough of it to give it a name. As he accepted defeat and followed his human into the office, he couldn't resist the feeling that it was something he was supposed to alert for.

Going into the office, Albert was already convinced they were barking up the wrong tree. The Simmons may or may not be unpleasant people, he hadn't seen any evidence to suggest they were deliberately targeting their rivals – other than the odd dig at their quality. It was no worse than Donna said about them every chance she got. However, he figured he might as well play along for a little bit longer, get his pie, and be on his way tomorrow.

That was until he walked into the small office.

The office was like offices in factories everywhere. This one was tidier because it was in a food manufacturing environment, but it had been designed to never be seen by customers. The office itself was about the size of a portacabin; roughly thirty feet by ten and the desks were arranged to look out over the factory floor which left the back wall free to be covered in charts.

It was the back wall, Albert found himself staring at. Or, more accurately, the staff organisation chart and the ten by eight picture of their employee of the month in the top right corner.

'What is it?' hissed Donna, wondering why the old man had frozen to the spot.

Of course, thought Albert, she hasn't seen the photograph yet. Taking out his phone, he advanced across the room to point at the employee of the month just as he got the email file to open. 'That's Mark Whitehouse,' he told her, holding the phone up so she could see both pictures side by side.

'Oh, my God!' exclaimed Donna. 'I was right all along. They did plant the thumb!' She had her phone out and a thumb on the nine button half a second later.

'What's going on here?' asked a gruff man's voice from behind them.

Donna ignored him as her call connected. 'Hello? Yes, police please.'

'Are you supposed to be with the group?' He wore pristine white overalls and white wellington boots. His hair was in a net and he wore a face mask which made it difficult to be sure, but he looked like another Simmons brother.

'Hurry, please!' shouted Donna. 'We're at Simmons pork pie factory. They've killed someone. Get here quick!'

Just then, Toby's mum appeared behind him as he blocked the door. 'I lost two along the way,' she explained, then took in that they were in an office where they had no good reason to be. 'What are you doing in here?' she demanded.

Donna didn't bother with the fake man's voice when she pointed an accusing finger at her. 'You tried to put my mum's shop out of business! Well, I've caught you now.'

Toby's mum was squinting at Donna, tilting her head slightly and pursing her lips. 'Don't I know you?'

'Um, no,' Donna tried. It came out sounding weak and Albert was ready to accept they were busted already.

'Yes, I do,' insisted Toby's mum.

They were busted, but Rex chose that moment to make himself visible. His nose detected food the moment he went into the office. There was a cheese sandwich inside a lunchbox in the middle drawer of the left-hand desk. It had a chocolate biscuit with it if he wasn't much mistaken. He could get into it, but having got that far, he discovered the crusty crumbs of a previous sandwich under the desk. The last two minutes had been devoted to licking the flavour out of the carpet tiles.

'Ah! It's a dog!' yelled Toby's mum.

'What the hell's a dog doing in the factory?' The man in the overalls demanded. 'Oh, my lord, this is a serious breach. We'll have to shut down all production until we can do a full clean.'

Undeterred by the panic now ensuing in the doorway, Donna wasn't finished with her accusations. 'You planted a thumb in my mum's shop,' she raged.

Toby's mum wasn't listening, she was shouting for help.

The man in the overalls snarled, 'I think you'd both better come with me.' Then he made the mistake of taking a step forward.

The man's face was covered by a mask, which Rex didn't like. He also sounded aggressive, so when he invaded the space Rex considered to be his human's, Rex made it quite clear his behaviour wasn't acceptable.

One second everyone was talking at once, the next, everyone froze.

Especially the man.

Rex knew he could bark and make the man back off, but what was the fun in that? He discovered long ago that he could use humans as squeaky toys. During his training, they had him chase men with big padded arms. He was supposed to bite the arm. Where was the sense in that?

He always went for an ankle or the arm that wasn't padded. He never hurt anyone, well not much. But once, when the man ran away, he tripped and fell just as Rex lunged and Rex got a mouthful of something far softer. The reaction that day was much the same as now. If you bite an arm or a leg, they will fight to get you off. Bite the soft bits in their trousers and they stop moving completely.

Albert sighed and took a seat. He read about this in the dog's report after he found out why the Met Police were rehoming him.

'What's he doing?' asked Donna.

Albert explained. 'Pacifying the aggressor. This is not the usual technique used.'

'I'll bet it isn't,' she agreed with wide eyes.

'Help,' squeaked the man. He was still standing but he didn't look like he wanted to be. When he reached down toward the dog's face, Rex growled and twitched his jaw in warning. He would sit here until he was sure his human was safe.

'Let him go, Rex,' ordered Albert.

'Please,' added the man.

Voices were coming toward the office from outside in the factory. Toby's mum had raised the alarm and more people were coming to help.

Hearing them, Rex decided his human's instruction probably no longer counted.

'Can you get your dog to let go?' begged the man.

'No, probably not,' Albert sighed again.

'What's his name,' asked the man, trying to be as quiet and as unthreatening as possible.

'It's Rex, but from where you are, you might want to think of him as Mr Dog.'

The voices outside arrived. It was one of the Simmons brothers from the front counter plus Toby. They all looked angry at being invaded, but it was going to get worse.

'Donna!' cried Toby, recognising her instantly despite the disguise. To be fair, the beard was peeling off badly on one side now. 'Oh, my God,

45

you insane hose beast. You want to know why I stopped calling? It's this. You are full bore bonkers, chick.'

Seeing no need to continue the pretence, Donna tore off the beard and wig. A chunk of the beard stayed on which made her look like a partially transformed, scruffy werewolf, but she was jabbing a finger at the employee of the month picture.

'Did you kill him on the premises? The police are on their way, you know,' she announced with a triumphant sneer. 'You shouldn't have targeted my mum's shop. You're all for it now!'

The elder Simmons man bore the same confused look as the rest of his family. 'Kill who? What is going on? Toby is this that girl you dated for a while last year and then dumped because you said she had wonky boobs?'

Donna gasped. 'Wonky … I do not.' Toby made the mistake of laughing which almost got him a slap as Donna swung her hand at his face.

'We're a little off subject, I fear,' Albert calmly reminded her as he caught her arm. Turning to address the Simmons family, he said, 'You employ Mark Whitehouse, yes?'

Mr Simmons narrowed his eyes but said, 'Yes.'

The man in the overalls said, 'Um, I still have a dog attached to me.' Rex twitched his jaw again with a quiet, low growl. 'And that's absolutely fine,' the man added, while sucking in air between his teeth and wincing.

'It was Mark Whitehouse's thumb that was found across the street in Agnew's Perfect Pork Pie Emporium.'

Albert's announcement drew a gasp from everyone in the Simmons family including the man in the overalls, although his gasp might have been one of pain.

46

More voices from outside heralded the arrival of yet more people. These ones Albert recognised. It was Detective Sergeant Moss and Detective Constable Wright and they did not look happy to see him.

Amidst a great deal of complaining from the Simmons family, the investigation was moved from the office on the factory floor to a different office above the shop. Upstairs was reserved for bookkeeping and non-food-related tasks so they could be there with the dog and not contaminate the factory further. Seeing that everyone wanted to leave, Rex Harrison finally let the man go, chuckling to himself about how effective his techniques were.

Moss and Wright had been on their way to The Pork Pie Palace when the call came through from dispatch. They showed as responding but hadn't expected the palaver awaiting them.

'Yes,' said DS Moss. 'We identified the owner of the thumb this morning. When he wasn't at home, we came to his place of work to ask if they had heard from him.'

Albert nodded. 'Solid policework.'

'Thank you,' she replied, not caring one bit what the old man thought. 'Why were you here and how did you know who the thumb belonged to?'

'Yeah,' echoed Toby. 'Why were you and wonky snooping around in our factory? Trying to sabotage it, I bet.'

His father gave him side eye. 'They think we killed Mark, dummy. That's why they were here. They already told us that.'

'Oh, yeah,' Toby fell quiet.

Albert, one of the only people sitting, explained about following the tattoo.

Moss couldn't deny that it was a clever way to track down the thumb's owner. 'That still doesn't explain why you were here. You admitted that you didn't know he worked here until you saw the picture,' she pointed out.

'No. Our presence here was guess work,' he admitted.

'Good guesswork,' insisted Donna. 'They've been trying to ruin my mum's business ever since they opened up shop.'

'No, we haven't.' Mrs Simmons sounded horrified at the idea. 'Have we?' she then asked, sounding less certain.

Mr Simmons pulled a face. 'There were a couple of early campaigns where we made negative comparisons to our biggest rival.' Seeing Donna draw a breath, he quickly added,' That was with a marketer who we quickly parted company from. I mean, you should see it as a compliment, really. Your firm is so big and established. Emporium's pork pies are the marker for the rest of the market.'

Mollified a little, Donna still wasn't letting them off the hook that easy. 'What about when you cut our power?' she snapped.

Albert noticed that DS Moss was quite content to watch the interplay. It was something he often did as a detective. No need to ask questions when everyone is throwing information around. You can just listen and see what revelations are laid bare.

'That wasn't us,' Mr Simmons insisted before seeing his son look guiltily at the floor. 'What did you do?' Mr Simmons asked with a tone of resigned acceptance.

'Well, it was her fault.' Toby pointed an accusing finger at Donna.

'Me?' Donna put her hands on her hips. 'How is it my fault you shut off the electricity to mum's shop. You cost us a day's takings.'

'You shouldn't have posted things about me on social media,' Toby hissed. 'You know what you wrote.'

Donna grinned like the Cheshire Cat. 'Oh, you mean about your tiny todger?'

'It's not tiny!' Toby shouted.

DS Moss made her presence felt. 'I think that's enough. Mr Simmons do you wish to press charges for trespass?'

'Yes, we do,' Toby answered first.

Mr Simmons shook his head. 'No. No, I don't want to do that.' He made eye contact with Donna. 'I don't know how Mark's thumb got into your premises, but it wasn't by our doing. If we can help your business to get back on its feet, then just let me know.' Then he puffed out his cheeks and turned back to look at DS Moss. 'I guess we know why Mark didn't show up for work last night. Do you think he is dead?'

DS Moss didn't answer his question. 'He hasn't been found yet. He might be receiving treatment somewhere and lying low. I will let you know when we find him. I need to ask you some questions before I go, but I think we should escort Mr Smith and Miss Agnew from the premises first.

Albert knew this bit was coming. He pushed himself out of the chair with a groan and to the percussion accompaniment of a click from each knee. 'Come along, Rex.'

Outside, having left her junior partner, Wright, to stay with the Simmons family, DS Moss had a stern warning. 'I could arrest you both. Of course, you already knew that when you chose to go snooping, didn't you, Mr Smith?' Albert nodded his head. 'This is a police matter and will be investigated by the police. You may have been a fine detective in your day; however, your day is long past and right now you are nothing more than an interfering old busybody. If I have cause to speak with you again, I will arrest you. Am I understood?'

Albert gave her a tight smile. He remembered saying almost exactly the same to a chap once many years ago. Now he was on the receiving end and got to find out what it felt like. 'Loud and clear, Detective Sergeant. There'll be no more trouble from me.'

DS Moss turned her attention to Donna. 'That goes for you too, Miss Agnew. I understand your desire to prove the thumb didn't arrive in your delivery of meat but that does not give you the right to start poking your nose into my investigation.'

'They are lying to you,' Donna insisted. 'You can't believe anything they say. They probably put Mark into the meat mixer and the evidence got eaten already.'

DS Moss seemed to consider that for a second, then dismiss it. She dug into a pocket and gave them each a card. 'I don't want to see either of you anywhere near this case again unless you have information I can use.' She didn't wait for an answer, walking back to the Simmons establishment without another word.

Donna said a rude word. 'I need to get this glue off my face,' she huffed, picking at the bits of beard still stuck to her. 'I guess that's it then.'

Albert raised an eyebrow. 'Oh, I don't think we should give up just yet. It's beginning to get interesting.'

Donna gawped at the old man. 'But the lady cop said she would arrest us.'

'Only if she catches us doing something,' Albert reminded her. 'But it occurred to me that I have never been arrested. It might be quite fun to find out what that is like.'

Donna continued to gawp. 'You're going to keep on snooping around?'

'I think I will,' Albert replied with a throwaway smile. Then he fixed a more serious expression on his face. 'You can call it detective's intuition if you like, but I think there is something going on here. You might not like it, but I think the Simmons family are innocent. Whether they are or not,' he added quickly when he saw Donna open her mouth to speak, 'a man is missing, and he left an important part of himself behind. Thumbs do not just get torn off by accident. I think someone tore it off and Mark is either dead, or he is hiding from those who did it.'

'That's horrible,' murmured Donna with a sickened expression.

'There are horrible people out there,' agreed Albert with a nod. 'I feel like getting some lunch. Why don't you get yourself changed back into your normal attire and come find me when you are done?'

'Where will you be?'

Pub Lunch

The Land Lover public house sat at the centre of the town's busy business district. Surrounded by shops selling clothes, jewellery, shoes, chocolate, and all manner of other goods. It had been on the same spot with the same name for a hundred and eighty-seven years. Albert popped in there on a whim yesterday when the pork pie class went out the window and in so doing, discovered one of those remarkable places one remembers until their deathbed.

It sported the most amazing menu of olde-world English food. Cumberland pie, steak and kidney pudding, Lancashire hotpot, faggots and mushy peas, the list went on. Albert thought he could stay for a month sampling a dish every day and never need to venture elsewhere.

Yesterday it had been the fish and chips that stole his heart, and though tempted to order it again, he forced himself to explore a different option. Today it was the steak and kidney pudding which was unbelievably filling. Encrusted in thick suet pastry, the pudding could easily have fed two which is why Rex Harrison got so much of it.

Rex happily took morsel after morsel as they were handed down. It was tasty, though no better than the raw meat he snagged in the class when no one was looking. He could never understand why humans felt such need to faff around with their food before they ate it. It was just as good before they started. His thoughts kept drifting back to the smell in the factory. Overwhelmed by pork pies as they baked, he couldn't put his paw on what the other smell was. It was going to drive him nuts until he worked it out.

Once his belly was full, Albert pushed back his seat a little. His trousers felt tight – it was a gut-buster of a portion - maybe he should rethink the policy of pub lunches.

Feeling clever, he called his youngest son. Albert had three children: Gary, the eldest at fifty-four, Selina, in the middle at fifty-one, and Randall, their surprise addition who turned forty-one last month. All had followed him into the police.

The call connected, Randall's voice coming onto the line, 'Is that you, Dad? Where are you?'

'I'm in a pub in Melton Mowbray.'

'Ah, yes. Leg one of your gastronomic tour of the British Isles. Cumberland next, isn't it?'

'Bakewell,' Albert corrected. 'Listen, Randall,' he changed his voice to serious. 'I have a favour to ask.'

'Shoot.'

'I need you to look up a file for me?'

There was a beat of silence at the other end. 'Dad, are you snooping again?'

Why did all his children ask him that? 'I'm just helping someone out,' he protested. 'It's just a small thing. A thumb was found last night. It belongs to a chap called Mark Whitehouse. Can you check in the central database and see if forensics turned up anything that night tell me where it was before it was found in a pork pie shop?'

'It was found in a pork pie shop? His son repeated. 'Well, I guess that tells me how you came to find out about it. Is the rest of him in the pork pies?'

'Hopefully not. They did shut the shop just in case, though, while they check the meat and the baked products. I would like to help the owners prove how it got onto their premises if I can. It might help the police here too,' he added.

'Okay, dad. I'll let you know when I have something.'

Albert placed his phone back on the table. His Randall was a good boy. All his kids were, but it was hard not to think of his youngest as his favourite. The elder brother and sister were too old to play with Randall by the time he was big enough to play and had been the butt of their practical jokes for much of his childhood. Still single in his forties, Albert worried he was too keen to advance his career and might miss out on having a family of his own if he didn't hurry up and find a girl soon.

Approaching feet turned out to be a waitress coming to collect his plate. Donna was right behind her, joining Albert at a spare chair. She was back in her own clothes, which today was blue skinny jeans, white converse high-tops, with a hoody on top. The hoody was bright red and branded with a sporting goods logo.

'What do we do now?' she asked.

It was a good question, but he thought of an answer. 'You said your mum installed CCTV cameras that look over the yard. Did the police confiscate the tapes?'

Donna snorted a laugh, amused by the old man's choice of phrase. 'It's all electronic. They downloaded the file to the cloud. I still have a copy. I can access it here on my phone.'

Albert didn't know that was a thing that could be done. He'd heard of the cloud but had no idea what it was or how it worked. Nevertheless, thirty seconds later, they were huddled together over Donna's phone as she scrolled through the footage from two nights ago.

The feed was a little grainy and the darkness meant it looked more black and white than the full colour spectrum it was undoubtedly shot in. Donna used a finger to advance the footage until something happened. A shadow appeared but she was moving too fast and had to back up. They both focussed harder to see what it was as she moved ever so slowly backwards.

'It's a cat,' sighed Albert.

Rex popped his head up. 'Where?'

Donna moved on again, past midnight, past one in the morning. Then she caught it, lifting her finger the moment he appeared. Even on her tiny screen, they could both tell it was Mark Whitehouse they were looking at from the moonlight shining off his head. His right hand looked to be wrapped in something and he cradled it with his left as he ran. He came over the wall at the rear of the property to land in the yard and ran directly toward the back of the pork pie shop. There he vanished from view as the camera angle lost him, but he reappeared a moment later running across the roof of a low extension.

'That's where we cut the meat!' Donna's excited outburst caught the attention of other patrons who all looked their way before drifting back to their drinks. Albert and Donna both saw the same thing: Mark Whitehouse tripped and fell as he ran across the rooftop. It was a flat roof and had two skylights in it.

'Is that one open?' Albert asked, poking his finger at it.

Donna shook her head. 'It's not supposed to be.'

'I think we might have just found out how the thumb got into the meat. We should go and look.'

'But there's police tape all over the front door,' Donna didn't think getting arrested sounded fun at all.

'Is there tape on the back door?'

Albert knew that the lack of crime scene tape warning people to stay out would form not the slightest defence if they were caught. The front of the building made it very clear no one was to go inside, and they had both been verbally advised by a police officer to stay away.

Around the back of the business, easily accessed by following the road around the corner, Albert let Rex off the lead so he could find a spot to do some watering if he needed.

'Don't wander off, Rex.'

Rex heard what his human said but wasn't paying any attention. He remembered the way the thumb smelled; old engine oil, gasoline and WorkSafe gloves. Here in the rear courtyard of the pork pie shop, he could smell it again only it was stronger this time. He checked over his shoulder; the humans were messing about by the back door. Deciding they were probably able to entertain themselves for a while, he left them to it, setting off back the way he came to follow his nose. It never let him down.

Donna had a key, but she really didn't want to get caught going in. Albert agreed it would be tantamount to tampering. 'How about if I climb on top and check it that way?' she asked.

'You'll be going by yourself,' he assured her. Donna wasted no time in getting onto the roof. It was only about eight feet up and a wheelie bin the business used made a handy boost to get half the way. No sooner did her head breach the edge of the roof than she saw how it must have happened.

One of the skylights wasn't fully closed. She would have to get angry with Alan and Jacob - they knew they had to close the vents. Closer inspection revealed a bloody mark around the open skylight and marks where the detritus of decades had been disturbed by someone scrambling around on it.

He had fallen, dropped the thumb he was carrying, and fate laughed in his face as it let the digit drop through the tiny gap in the skylight. There was supposed to be mesh on the other side, but as she got her face down to look through the gap, she could see it had torn. With a tut, she thought about how many little things needed to be done better when they reopened.

If they reopened, she reminded herself and then told herself off for being negative.

The thumb dropping through the skylight still didn't explain how it got into the meat which would be locked away inside the refrigerators at that time of night. That was a question for another time. Being careful to avoid getting her clothes mucky, she took pictures with her phone to show Albert, then stood up to see beyond the back wall. She'd never thought about it before: what lay beyond the back wall. She knew there was another street with businesses, rather than houses, behind them, and now she could see the backs of the buildings.

It didn't tell her much.

A couple of doors along was a mechanic's yard. That one was easy to spot because it had a roller door and cars in various stages of repair. She watched for a minute but couldn't see any activity inside or outside the business. The other businesses were less easy to identify because there was nothing displayed on this side. She took another picture and then climbed back down.

Albert kept the wheelie bin steady as Donna clambered over the top of it to drop back lightly onto her feet.

'There's a bloody mark by the skylight. I think that is how the thumb ended up inside though it couldn't have fallen through and into the meat.' Something occurred to her as she made the remark. It made her pause, but she filed it away for later consideration.

'You were saying?' Albert prompted.

Shaking her head as a physical action to remove her mental train of thought, Donna brought herself back to the task at hand. 'I think we can be sure the thumb getting inside was an accident. I guess I owe the Simmons an apology; they didn't plant it after all.'

Albert noticed that Donna had stopped talking again, she seemed even more distracted this time, looking around the yard and leaning to the side to peer behind where he stood.

'Where's your dog?' she asked.

Rex wasn't far away, in fact. He'd only walked twenty yards beyond the rear courtyard of the pork pie shop. It was far enough for him to reach the rear of the mechanic's place where his nose was now going wild. This place definitely smelled just like the thumb. There were all manner of other smells mixed up in it too. Rat poop was on the list, which meant there had to be rats and they were fun to chase. He could smell new tyres, cigarettes, coffee, and someone had recently cut themselves quite badly because the heavy, metallic tang of blood was ripe on the air. He could smell what the mechanics had for lunch and the cologne the old woman on the reception desk wore.

Then … there was something else in there. Mixed in with the old oil and tobacco. Something …

'Rex!'

Oops.

'Rex!'

His human was shouting in a worried manner. Not that Rex thought there was anything to worry about. He hurried back to where he left them anyway. 'I am here,' he announced with a chuffing noise as he rounded the corner to re-enter the courtyard.

Albert breathed a sigh of relief, momentary panic spiking his heartrate when he saw the dog had wandered away. It was his fault, of course. The dog couldn't be blamed for wandering off when left untethered. 'Good, dog,' he praised as the big hairy animal danced about in front of him.

'I've found something. I've found something,' said Rex excitedly, attempting to impart that he thought he knew what this was all about now. 'It's just down here. I couldn't smell it correctly at first because there were too many other smells mixed in with it but just come with me and I will show you.'

Donna placed her hand on her knee as she bent down to ruffle Rex's fur. 'I wonder what has got him so animated.'

Albert chuckled. 'He's probably solved the crime all by himself.' Donna showed Albert the pictures she took: the bloody print and the back of the businesses. They knew he came over the wall from the place directly behind, so they were heading around to see what sort of business it was.

Rex just stared at them both. 'Really? You're not getting any of this? Can't you smell it? It stinks of blood, it smells just like the thumb did, and it's got that other weird smell that they used to make me search for. They always wanted me to alert when I found it. Do you need me to do that now? Will that help?

'What's he doing now?' asked Donna, staring at the dog.

'Damned if I know?' Albert wanted to go around to the next street where they could scope out the businesses. Mark Whitehouse had been there for a reason and returned missing a thumb. To Albert, it felt like they were closing in, but now his dog wouldn't move and was barking like a mad thing.

'What is it, Rex?' asked Donna.

Rex stopped barking to look in her eyes. 'I'm glad you asked. I believe what you are looking for is directly behind this wall. If you would be so kind as to open this door, I will lead you to the source of the smell.' Thankful he was finally getting through; he noted the need to signal an alert if he wanted to get their attention.

Albert gave his lead another gentle tug. 'Come along, Rex. We need to go this way.'

Donna squinted at the dog. 'He wants to go through that door.' She jumped on the spot to look over the wall. 'It's a mechanic's yard,' she said.

Albert shrugged and gave Rex's lead a more insistent tug. 'He can probably smell food. Or he saw a cat.' Rex dug his claws in. 'Come on, Rex,' he begged. 'We can't go in that way.'

Oh, thought Rex. I hadn't considered that. You probably don't have a key. 'Let's go around the front,' he said with his chuffing noise as he started to lead the way. Tugging his human along as he powerwalked along the street, he continued to describe what he could smell. 'This would be so much easier if you would just use your noses.'

The business behind the pork pie shop was a bookies. A large, backlit sign in green with white letters announced Grand Turf Accountant. Standing in front of it, Donna noted the position of the mechanic's yard, the one business she could easily identify from the back and counted off - the turf accountant place was definitely the one that backed onto her mum's pork pie shop.

'This is it,' she announced.

Albert had never been a gambler. It didn't tempt him anyway, but he saw too many people driven to crime to pay off debts they ought to never have amassed because they thought they could beat the odds. Was that what happened to Mark?

Scratching his head as he looked at the business's front façade, Albert summed up what was bothering him. 'Mark was the night-watchman for a pork pie factory. With a criminal record, it seems a surprising job to obtain, but he got it. However, two nights ago he wasn't guarding the factory, he was climbing over the wall and into your mum's place with his thumb missing. The bookies, in fact none of the businesses around here are open at one in the morning, so where was he coming from?'

Donna hadn't thought about that. 'Where could he have been? Why go over the wall at all?'

'Because he was being chased,' Albert concluded.

By his feet, Rex waited patiently. They were nearly at the mechanic's place when they stopped. Humans got up to all kind of strange activities that he didn't understand, so he let it pass, certain they would move on soon enough.

'Why would he be at a bookies at night?' Albert asked a rhetorical question. 'This is a privately owned bookkeepers, not one of the big national franchises, and that means local ownership. Maybe our man ran up a debt and was lured here so they could incentivise him to pay it off.'

Donna grimaced when she asked, 'You think they pulled off his thumb to make him pay up?'

Albert thought back to some of the bodies he had seen over the years. 'Ninety percent of crime is committed because of money or sex. People get into bookkeeping because they want to be rich, and the gambling industry is a cold ruthless world. It wouldn't shock me at all to find out he was up to his eyeballs in debt.'

Donna was beginning to get second thoughts about snooping around now. If they were capable of pulling off thumbs, she really didn't want to meet them. 'I think maybe this is getting a little more dangerous than I imagined. Perhaps I ought to call it quits, patch things up with Belinda and see how quickly I can get the health inspector to let me reopen.'

Albert didn't want to sway her either way, but he said, 'We're here now. We might as well go inside and have a look around.' At that moment, the door opened and a pair of men in their forties walked out, pocketing winnings they had just collected and laughing over a shared joke.

Albert started toward the still closing door. Rex frowned; he wanted to go to the mechanic's business two doors down. Did he argue now, or let it go? Choosing to go with his human as long as they got to the mechanic's place soon, he followed them inside.

Just above head height for the humans, were a dozen televisions displaying horse racing, football matches, and other sports, or advertising ways to win big with various complicated betting methods. It had all changed vastly since Albert last came into a betting shop. Back then, when he was still a policeman, it was all done on slips of paper. Now it appeared to be electronic and the punters could lose their money directly from a credit card if they wanted. Dotted around the room, many of them back to back, were fruit machine sized betting stations. Each had a large screen with the words, 'Touch screen to begin,' emblazoned on it.

Seeing the new technology, Albert chose to take advantage of his honest confusion. There was a man working behind a counter at the far end of the office. He wore a shirt and tie, but no jacket. His beer belly stuck out over his belt to obscure the button and a roll of fat hung over his collar from his neck. His face was lit up by the computer screen he stared at, but he wore a name badge with Grand Turf Accountants at the top.

'I say,' said Albert, quickly glancing at a screen above his head.

The man's eyes flicked up. Albert waved. 'I say, could I get a little help?'

Energised, as if for the first time today he finally had something to do, the man left his station. With a broad smile, he approached. 'Yes, of course. What is it that I can help you with?'

Albert glanced again at the screen above his head. 'I came in with my granddaughter to place a bet, but it's all a little confusing.'

Rex got bored and spread himself out on the carpet tile to rest.

Colin, the name badge declared his name, was only too happy to help. 'It's all quite easy once you get the hang of it.' He leaned across to tap the screen, which made it jump to a new screen. 'You simply select the type of sporting event you want to bet on,'

'It's a horse race,' Albert told him. 'The two o'clock at Edgbaston. I have a hot tip from a friend who comes in here all the time.'

'Oh, really?' asked Colin pressing the screen to take him to the runners for the two o'clock race. 'Which horse is it?'

Albert had memorised one from looking at the screen above his head. 'Three-legged nag.'

Colin's eyebrows did a dance before he got them back under control. 'Righto. Three-legged Nag at one hundred and fifty to one. Do you want that each way?'

'Each way what?' asked Albert, confused by the betting term.

'That just means you win if he comes in first or second,' Donna clarified.

'Oh, ah, yes. I think that's what Mark said to do. Maybe you know him,' said Albert getting to the bit of the conversation he had been steering for. From his pocket, he pulled out his phone and his reading glasses.

Colin wasn't paying any attention; he was loading up the bet. 'That's Three-legged Nag in the two o'clock at Edgbaston each way. How do you want to pay?'

Caught out by how fast it all was, Albert ground his teeth and took out his wallet. 'Oh, it looks like I spent all my cash at lunchtime.'

'Not to worry,' said Colin, cheerily. 'We have an ATM in the corner.'

Albert tracked Colin's eyes. 'Oh, yes. So you do.'

'You can just put your card in here though.' Colin pointed to a slot below the screen. You just have to tell it how much to take first. Then it will ask for your card.'

Seeing no way out now, Albert grumbled in his head and took out his debit card. 'What's the minimum bet?' he asked.

'Oh, you never want to go with the minimum,' advised Colin. He had a salesman's smile of friendly confidence fixed in place – *I'm your best friend and I would never steer you wrong.*

Albert eyed him cautiously. 'I don't?'

'Goodness, no. Think about it like this. How much can you afford to lose?' None at all, thought Albert. 'Let say you pick ten pounds. You lose ten pounds, it's no big deal; that's not even enough for a takeaway and a bottle of wine. But if that horse wins, you get fifteen hundred bucks.'

'Really?' said Donna, suddenly taking interest at the number displayed on the screen as, 'Potential winnings'.

Colin reached across to tap a different number. 'Now, let's say, instead of ten pounds you bet thirty.' A new number flashed up. 'Suddenly, you have enough for a Caribbean holiday. Gamble responsibly; that's our motto here. Only ever bet what you can afford to lose, but never lose sight of what you stand to win. Otherwise, why bet at all?'

Albert knew it was a con, but he hadn't got the information he came in here for yet and was beginning to feel that he was going to have to place a bet just to move things along.

Seeing the old man was at tipping point, Colin gave him a gentle nudge, 'You said your friend gave you a hot tip?''

Seizing the chance to get the conversation back under control, he tucked his open wallet under his arm and brought his phone up to eye height again. Even with his reading glasses on, he needed to move his head back and forth until the picture was in focus. 'His name is Mark

Whitehouse.' Albert turned the phone around to show Colin the headshot. 'He comes in here all the time. Do you know him? Does he win big, or was he yanking my chain?'

Colin's forehead creased. 'I don't think I have ever seen him before. Sorry.'

Albert shifted position and his wallet slipped. He caught it again by clenching his arm but the wallet had come to rest by his elbow and right above the machines payment scanner.

It beeped.

'What was that?' asked Albert.

'You just placed your bet,' beamed Colin, content that he had just made thirty pounds from the old man. Who on earth place a bet of any size against a horse called Three-legged Nag?

'But I hadn't finished deliberating,' Albert complained as the machine spat out a receipt.

'Oh, I'm sorry,' replied Colin, not meaning a word of it. 'All bets are final.'

'Can I increase my bet?' asked Albert warily.

'Yes, of course you can increase it.' Colin was having a great time with the crazy old man. 'How much shall we say? A hundred on the nose this time,' he prodded the machine back into life and started pressing buttons. 'I just need the receipt number to add more funds to your wager.'

Albert narrowed his eyes at the tubby man. 'I thought you said all bets were final.'

Seeing the trap too late, Colin felt his face heat up a little. 'Well, you can always bet more money ...'

'But I can't decrease or cancel my bet.' Albert finished Colin's sentence for him. None of this was a surprise to Albert, he never thought of gambling as a sensible hobby. People made fools of themselves from other people only too happy to let people be foolish. 'Come along, Donna. I think we should be on our way.'

'Come back any time,' Colin called jovially.

At the doorway, Albert paused, 'Young man, I shall be back for my winnings.'

'Now can we go to the mechanic's yard?' asked Rex. His human patted his skull and fussed the fur behind his ear.

'Well that was a bust,' said Albert.

Donna frowned her lack of understanding. 'Because he said he didn't know Mark? What if he was lying?'

'He wasn't.' Albert shook his head. 'If you watch a person's face, it is easy to tell if they are lying or not. Colin had never seen Mark Whitehouse before. I think we should assume it wasn't the bookkeepers he was running away from.'

They both took a minute to scan down the other businesses facing them on the small parade of shops. To the left of the bookkeeper's was a boutique hairdressing salon.

Albert and Donna looked at each other. 'No,' they said in unison.

To the left of that was a shop selling bathrooms and plumbing products which seemed just as unlikely. To the bookkeeper's right was a fast food franchise and to the right of that a car repair place.

Donna puckered her lips and blew out a breath. 'This really is a bust. I can't see why he would be in any of these places late at night, let alone losing his thumb.'

Between pork pie making classes, police interviews, a pub lunch, and their snooping, there wasn't much afternoon left. Albert wasn't hungry, but he had been on his feet quite a bit and he was feeling it in his knees and hips. More than anything, he felt he needed time to think about what he might have missed.

'I think maybe we should call it a day,' he suggested.

Rex swung his head upward in disbelief. 'What? It's right there. You humans need to stop trusting your eyes. I can smell the blood from here.'

Donna crouched down to see why Rex was making all the chuffing noises. He was up on his feet and straining at his lead, backing away toward the mechanic's place in a bid to drag the two humans that way. Maybe if they got close enough, even their handicapped noses might detect the obvious smells.

'No, Rex,' Albert chided. 'It's time to go home. Or back to the B&B at least.'

Accepting that the humans were not going to get it, he ducked his head, so his collar slipped up to the base of his ears, and then gave a yank. His head popped free as he knew it would.

'Right, dummies,' Rex Harrison barked loudly as he bounded along the pavement. 'This way to solve a crime.' It saddened him a little that his human needed to be led by the hand all the time. He found it the same when he was in the police. They said he had a bad attitude, but he wouldn't have if they ever listened to him. They would run around talking to people when all they needed to do was smell the evidence.

Just then his nose caught scent of something he couldn't resist. It caused his head to snap around where across the road, a lady dalmatian was going for a walk with her human. With the smell she kicked out, there was no way for him to ignore the call.

'Hey, babe,' he called nonchalantly as he sashayed across the street.

Behind him, his human and the young woman who started hanging out with him yesterday, were calling his name and chasing after him, but he could barely hear them over the hammering rush of blood in his head.

The dalmatian swung her head to see who wanted her attention, then flipped him a come-and-get-it-grin. 'Oh, yeah, big boy? Think you've got what it takes do you?'

She stopped walking, which jerked her human's arm. 'Hey, Mitzy!' said the human. Then she spotted Rex approaching. 'Oh, no you don't! Go away you bad dog!'

'Bad dog? Oh, lady, I am going to be so good for your Mitzy. Can't you tell how bad she wants it?'

Mitzy was trying to turn around. She didn't really understand why she got like this. Most of the time she had no interest in boy dogs at all. Then every few months, they were all she could think about for a week.

Mitzy started whining sweet nothings as Rex approached, but her human was still trying to drag her along the pavement. 'Bad dog, Mitzy. Bad dog!'

'Oh, I hope you are,' growled Rex, really getting into the mood now.

'Gotcha,' Albert declared triumphantly as he snagged the collar back over Rex's head.

'No!' shrieked Rex. 'No! We just need a few minutes. We can do it right here. We won't run off.'

Albert apologised to the dalmatian's owner. 'Sorry about that. Daft brute slipped his collar.'

'Perhaps it should be tighter,' snapped the dalmatian's owner.

'Miiiitzyyyy!' Rex howled as she was dragged away.

Mitzy accepted defeat, blowing Rex a kiss as her owner got to a corner. 'I'll remember you always.'

Albert was out of breath from running to catch Rex, doubled over and leaning on a car, he asked, 'Donna, could you be a sweet and tighten his collar?'

'Um, sure,' Donna knelt to fiddle with the latch around Rex's neck.'

Rex glared at his human. 'I am not talking to you and I am not helping with your silly investigation. Solve it by yourself, you ungrateful noseless human.' Feeling that wasn't enough, he vowed to sleep under the bed tonight and fart as much as he could.

Task complete, Donna straightened up again. 'I take it you haven't had him … you know … done.' She mimed cutting fruit from a tree.

Rex's eyes widened.

Albert puffed out his cheeks. 'Lightening his trouser department? Not yet. It always seemed like a cruel thing to do.' Hearing that, Rex leaned his head against his human's leg. 'I'm thinking it might not be a bad idea now, of course.'

Rex narrowed his eyes and thought about lifting his leg on a certain someone's trousers.

Donna stared across the street at the row of businesses again. 'Before he saw the dalmatian, I swear he was trying to get to the mechanic's place.'

It was getting late. Albert thought the walk back to the B&B might finish him off, but they were already here, and it wouldn't do any harm to check it out.

A Clue

The car repair place bore the name Blakes Auto Repairs above a small office. Made as cheaply as possible, the sign, cut from sheet steel and painted, was hand-made, which probably explained the missing apostrophe. Albert wondered how they got customers into the place when it looked so cheap from the outside. It looked more like a breaker's yard where cars came to die, than an auto-repair shop where professionally trained mechanics breathed new life into tired engines and performed mechanical surgery to keep them running safely.

The front yard had once been laid with tarmac, but erosion, weeds, and heavy traffic had reduced most of it to gravel. It would be pocked with puddles whenever it rained but in the dry it was just a craggy, oil-stained surface.

'Hello?' said the old woman sitting at the reception desk. She was frowning at Albert and Donna as if they had walked into her house and were trespassing. Her attitude mirrored the crappy façade and impoverished surroundings.

'Yes, hello. I was hoping to book my car in for a tune up,' said Albert having thought up the lie only moments before.

'Most people just phone,' the woman replied, not moving her hands to touch the keyboard.

'We were walking by,' he explained with a congenial smile.

Rex was on high alert. Now that he was inside the place, his nose was going nuts. There was blood here, but it was a couple of days old and the scent of bleach made him think the humans must have been trying to clean it up. He really needed to get into the garage bit where he could put his nose to work sorting through the underlying smells to find the source.

It wasn't just blood he could smell, the other thing, the thing they taught him to alert for was here too. He didn't know what it was called but they always got very excited when he found it and rewarded him with his favourite ball.

'I'm afraid we don't have any available spots this week,' the woman in reception told him, still not checking her computer, still not giving him her name.

'I'm Albert,' he told her to see how she might react.

'That's nice.' Her response dripped with sarcasm. Wherever she learned customer relations taught it very differently to everywhere else.

'Is there a need to be so rude?' asked Donna.

'Oh, look at the time,' said the woman, not glancing at the clock. 'It's five past overstayed your welcome.'

A door behind her desk with a poster of a topless young lady holding a shiny new exhaust pipe opened to reveal a man in a pair of grimy overalls. He had close-cropped hair going silver and his overalls were undone at the front where they couldn't accommodate his belly. 'Everything alright, Brenda?'

'I was hoping to get some repairs done,' Albert addressed the man directly.

'I thought you wanted a tune up,' snapped Brenda.

'Can you tell me if you can change the leaf springs on a mark three Ford Escort. It's the RS2000 version.'

'Sorry, no,' said the man. 'We don't have the equipment for that. You should try Pinner's on Almond Road. They ought to be able to help you.'

'Pinner's on Almond Road,' echoed Brenda forcefully. She was doing everything except shooing them out with a broom.

'You are not very nice,' observed Donna, coolly. She felt that the last couple of days, ever since finding the thumb, had been more stressful than they needed to be and now Brenda was being unpleasant without provocation. She felt like venting some of the frustration she felt, and Brenda was about to get both barrels.

'Thank you for your help.' said Albert, putting a hand on Donna's shoulder so he could steer her to the door.

'What?' said Donna. 'They didn't help us. That cow at the desk ...'

'What did you call me?' growled Brenda getting to her feet.

'I think it's time we left,' Albert suggested in a sing-song voice. 'I'll tell you why when we get outside.'

Too late, Donna was already responding to Brenda's question, 'I called you a cow. I was wrong to do that, please forgive me. I meant to say a big, fat, ugly cow!'

'Aahhhh!' Brenda ran around the side of her desk with a four-hole punch in her hands.

Rex, who had remained quiet until this point as he tried to sift the smells in his nose, did what he was trained to do and protected his principal. By extension that now included Donna.

Brenda hadn't noticed the large German Shepherd until she came around the desk and he was suddenly flying at her with his teeth showing as he barked in her face. Unable to stop her feet in time as she tried to correct her momentum, she fell onto her rump, dropping the four-hole punch which landed on the crown of her skull.

The old man, the girl, and the dog went back out the door, the dog giving her a final warning growl as he went.

'Why did we just leave?' asked Donna, trying hard not to sound upset with the old man who was so generously giving his time to help her investigate.

'Because it's a front.'

'A front?'

'Yes. They probably do fix cars, but that's not why that business exists. It is there so it looks like an auto-repair shop when it is really something else.'

'What else is it?' Donna asked, truly intrigued by the old man's claim.

Albert wrinkled his eyebrows. 'That I don't know. But I'll be willing to bet more than I wagered on that daft horse that this is where Mark lost his thumb. They have tools and things in there for a start.'

'How can you be so sure?'

'Well, for starters, Brenda had no intention of booking my car in for its annual test. She never once so much as glanced at her computer and no business employs someone that rude to work in reception if they want to stay in business. More convincing, though, was the mechanic's answer to my question.'

'About your imaginary Ford Escort?'

'Yes. That model doesn't have leaf springs. The manufacturer switched over to McPherson struts when they launched the mark three. Mark twos had leaf springs as did other models in the Ford line-up such as the Capri, and any mechanic on the planet would know that.'

Donna was trying to keep up with Albert. 'If that isn't a mechanic's shop, what is it?'

Stakeout

Fifty yards up the street two men in a car watched the old man and the young woman. 'Are they arguing?' asked the man in the passenger seat.

'Hard to tell,' said his partner. 'They look like they tried to get served and got spat out like everyone else.'

'Most criminals at least try to make their front businesses look and operate like a real business.' The first observed. His name was Terrance Torrance, a daft name that made everyone ask him to repeat himself when he said it. He always introduced himself as Terry to get around it. His partner's name was Silvio Draeger, a third generation Pole whose grandparents came to England after the war. Both were part of the National Drug Squad and bored with their current assignment. The Squad was after a drug manufacturer, but not only were they not able to work out where the drugs were being made, the criminals had a genius distribution method the police were unable to crack. It was getting to the street, the same product all over the country, but no one could work out how it was being shipped about without anyone knowing. The police kept thinking they were close but everywhere they ever raided turned out to be a false lead – it was run by the drug gang, but the police never found any drugs.

The current theory was the criminals were getting cleverer; they showed the cops where they were to entice them to raid. Only then, did the police discover there was nothing to be found because the cover operation was just a dummy to distract them and tie up their resources while the real operation took place somewhere else.

The woman, Brenda Crumb, was a small fish, they knew that much, and their boss wanted the big fish. No one knew who that was, though it was suspected that the crystal meth enterprise was part of a bigger network of supply with a fat cat crime lord sitting on top.

This was the fourth place Terrance and Silvio had staked out in the last month in their bid to find one that might have some actual drugs inside. It was another seven hours until they would be replaced, unless they were able to determine one way or the other if there was any manufacture going on here.

'I'm going for some pretzels,' announced Draeger. 'I need something salty. You want anything?'

'Hmmm?' Torrance had heard what his partner said but was too absorbed in watching the old man and the teenage girl arguing. At least he thought they were arguing. Sensing that Silvio was waiting for a response, he murmured, 'No, thanks, man. I'm all good.'

Silvio left the car, walking along the road to pass the old man and girl who were strangely talking about soap operas.

'Why did you just ask me what soap operas I like to watch?' Donna felt Albert's behaviour could be a little erratic and was starting to question if all his marbles were still in the bag.

Albert looked at her for a few seconds longer, just until he was confident the man was out of earshot. 'That's the other reason I know it's a front for a criminal enterprise.' Donna continued to stare at him; she had no idea what he was talking about. Albert put her out of her misery. 'The man that just passed us, please don't look. He is an undercover cop. His partner is parked in a silver Mondeo fifty yards up the road. I spotted them when we were coming out of the bookies. It's the extra antenna on the back of the car that gives it away.'

Donna glanced up the road, trying to be surreptitious about it. She would never have seen it, but the man sitting in the passenger seat of a silver Mondeo was so obviously a cop it was hard to imagine anyone missing it.

'Let's move away, shall we?' suggested Albert as he started moving.

Rex still wanted to get inside the mechanic's place. His plan had been to find the thing that was making his nose twitch and alert again. Even though the humans weren't able to smell it, surely they would be clever enough to understand he was showing them something?

Albert started to move but when the lead in his hand met with resistance, he didn't tug it to get the dog moving. Instead, he pursed his lips in thought and stared downward. The dog was looking up, making eye contact and seemingly trying to impart some message with his eyes.

'You want to go in there, don't you, boy?' asked Albert.

Rex jumped to his feet and wagged his tail.

Albert checked left and right, then reached down to unclip Rex's lead.

Rex paused for just a moment to be sure his lead was off. When he saw the loose end in his human's hand, he pushed off with his back legs and ran, steaming across the forecourt and into the mechanic's shop.

'Oh, dear. Rex seems to have got away from me again.'

Donna spun around. She hadn't seen Albert take the lead off. 'I'll get him.'

Albert touched her arm. 'He'll come back shortly. I have a hunch that he knows more than I realised.'

'What do you mean?' Donna and Albert both watched as the large German Shepherd whizzed into the workshop. Beyond the open roller door, four cars were visible. One was raised on a lift with a man poking about underneath it. An ageing BMW had its bonnet up and several parts from it were strewn on the concrete floor around it. Rex darted between them, his nose leading him as he shoved it into a toolbox, move quickly on and found a bench to sniff.

'I think he was alerting earlier.' Seeing his explanation required more detail, Albert said, 'The police dogs are taught all manner of behaviours to see where their aptitude is strongest. One of the behaviours is sniffing for drugs or explosives. I doubt this is explosives,' he added quickly.

'But it might be drugs,' Donna concluded.

Rex shouted, 'Bingo!'

'Wow! He's really going nuts.' Donna stood on her tip toes and strained to see what was getting Rex so excited. All she could see was his backend wagging like mad and the grimy mechanics getting excited about the dog in their workshop.

Brenda leapt out of her chair to see what caused the hullabaloo but heard the dog at the same time. Getting seen off by the dog just when she was going to teach that rude girl some manners had put her in a bad mood. Not that she was in a good mood beforehand with all the drama of the last few days. But when she saw the girl in the street with the old man, both looking inside while their dog caused a ruckus, she yelled for Mikey.

'Mikey!'

Mikey was trying to deal with the dog but couldn't decide whether the large beast was playing a game or genuinely dangerous. 'Go on! Get out of here!' he shouted, waving his arms but not getting too close. Mikey was a big man who knew how to handle himself. At forty-five he had learned enough dirty tricks that fights were over in seconds. That was against people though, not angry, snappy dogs with big teeth. Six feet two inches and two hundred and fifty pounds did not make any difference in these circumstances. His cousin Malcolm was even bigger, the two of them joining forces at a young age when they discovered their combined might would deter most rivals. Trim waists had given way to beer bellies over the years, but they still considered themselves to be formidable.

The dog danced about and barked some more. He was sniffing at the door that led to their storeroom. It was where they were keeping the product because they couldn't ship it at the moment. Mikey's yelling wasn't having any effect on the dog so when Malcolm arrived next to him, Mikey grabbed a large spanner, brandishing it like a weapon.

Rex saw the spanner and chuckled. 'If you try to hit me with that, I'm going to chew your feet off!' he barked a warning. Running into the workshop, he found the place that smelled like blood almost straight away. He could tell the thumb had been here, the place stunk of it – fear and sweat. Those were the underlying scents beyond the old engine oil and gasoline. They had been on the thumb and now they were here. The smell of blood was on the bench in the main part of the workshop and in a trash bin next to it. The scent they trained him to alert for was behind this door and it was stronger than ever now that he was able to get his nose into the gap at the bottom.

These men wanted him to go away which was incongruous. Normally the game of hide and seek resulted in a reward – often his favourite ball to play with. Why were they shouting at him now that he'd found the source of the scent? He alerted again just in case they hadn't understood him the first time.

Too scared to get any closer to the bonkers dog and his mouthful of teeth, Mikey threw the spanner.

Rex caught it. Eyeing the grimy man angrily, because he understood his intent was to harm, Rex bit down on the spanner and spat it out.

'Blimey, Mikey, he's bent it,' observed Malcolm as he backed away, finding a hefty toolbox to put between him and the dog. He was bigger than Mikey, but just as wary of the dog.

Brenda whacked Mikey on his arm. 'I have been shouting your name!' she growled.

Blinking at her, while cutting his eyes nervously back to the dog to see if it was staying put, Mikey said, 'Sorry, boss. I couldn't hear you with all the racket out here.'

Brenda glared at Malcolm. 'What are you doing? Are you hiding from a dog?'

Malcolm nodded his head vigorously. 'Damned skippy I am.'

'Get the oxyacetylene kit, you idiot!' she snapped. 'Scare the dog out with fire.'

In the street, Terrance Torrance arrived, skidding to a stop next to the old man and the cute girl. 'What the heck is going on?' he asked breathlessly.

'Ah, officer,' Albert addressed him casually. 'My ex-police dog appears to have found something of interest.'

Terrance blinked twice, stunned the old man knew he was a police officer, but far more concerned that months of police work were going up in smoke. 'We need to get him out of there! Right now!'

Albert said, 'No need to shout.' Frowning, he turned his attention back to the auto-repair centre. 'Rex!' he followed the shout with a whistle, but Rex had already decided it was time to leave. The human advancing with a nasty looking blue flame was a bit more than he felt like tackling today.

Bursting back out of the workshop through the gap between cars, he leapt over the bonnet of a parked Volvo to land the other side. It was an exuberant and unnecessary display of his athletic prowess, but he felt real joy – the last few minutes had been really fun.

'Good boy, Rex!' Albert ruffled his dog's fur and patted his flank. 'Good dog. Was that fun?'

Rex spun on the spot, wondering whether he should tear off to do another round of the workshop just for good measure. The click noise of his lead connecting to the loop in his collar killed that idea, but he still felt fired up and his human had found a new person to play with.

'Who are you?' Rex barked at the newcomer.

'Quickly. Come with me, please?' urged Terrance.

Coming up the street toward them was Silvio, confusion dominating his features as he tried to work out why his partner was out of the car and in plain sight of the business they were supposed to be staking out. 'What's going on?' he asked, unaware he had pretzel crumbs in his stubble and stuck to his lips.

Terrance wasted no time explaining, ushering the old man, the girl and the dog back along the street where they could sort out what was happening without the criminals in the fake repair shop watching them.

Squinting her eyes as they departed, Brenda growled at Mikey and Malcolm. 'I want those two followed. You understand. No one comes into my place and makes a fool of me.'

'Shouldn't we be packing up the gear?' asked Malcolm nervously; it didn't pay to question Brenda.

'I'll take care of that. You two idiots find out who the girl and the old man are.'

'What if they are police?' Malcolm persisted, taking his life into his own hands.

Brenda just sighed. 'Police? She's not old enough and he's two decades too old. He had to be eighty if he's a day. Stop trying to use your brain, Malcolm. You'll just hurt yourself. And then I'll hurt you,' she added for good measure.

Malcolm and Mikey knew better than to push their luck any further. They didn't want to end up like Mark.

Silvio caught up to his partner and the civilians still wondering what he managed to miss in the five minutes it took to go to the corner shop. Hours of boredom with nothing to look at and it all goes down the moment he stepped away. Typical.

Terrance stopped walking, his pace slower than he wanted in deference to the old man, but they were far enough away now. He needed to deal with this and hope the damage was minor.

Swivelling around to face the odd couple, a grandfather and granddaughter he assumed, he set his face to pleasant. 'You already seem to know that I am a police officer.'

Albert glanced over his shoulder to look back at the workshop. 'Don't you think we should be a little farther away. They are still watching us.'

'I know what I am doing,' Terrance assured him with a smile.

Albert's eyebrows rose without instruction. 'All evidence to the contrary, young man.' Donna sniggered which didn't help matters.

Terrance had taken all he could tolerate. Had the man been younger he might have grabbed his collar. Since he couldn't, and there were CCTV cameras everywhere these days, he dropped his voice an octave to issue a quiet threat. 'Listen, old man. There is a police investigation underway and you are interfering in it.'

'No,' Albert argued, quite aware of where he stood legally. 'I am a civilian going about my day. That I happened to stroll into a business that is clearly a front for some kind of drug manufacture ought not have been any concern of yours. Yes, my dog has been trained to sniff out drugs and that undoubtedly made them twitchy. However, you could have ignored it and maintained your cover. That would have been the right thing to do, but instead you barrelled into the situation, identifying yourself to the targets. To be fair, I spotted you the moment I came into the street, so I expect they knew you were here all along.'

Donna added, 'Your car sticks out a mile.'

Terrance and Silvio looked at the car. 'No, it doesn't,' argued Terrance. 'It's a silver Mondeo. There are hundreds of them around.'

'How many are fitted with an extra radio and antenna?' Albert was being argumentative for no good reason. The cops were just trying to do their job. He remembered what it was like: less well-resourced than the enemy, less free to move, always having to obey strict guidelines for engagement and chain of evidence. He softened his tone. 'Look, boys. We didn't mean to cause bother. We were just trying to book a tune up for my car and happened to wander by that place. Clearly it isn't what we thought it was, and you chaps have it well in hand. We'll be on our way.'

'Hold on,' Terrance held out an arm as the old man started to move. 'You said your dog is an ex-police dog and could smell drugs. What did he smell?'

Albert shrugged. 'You'll have to ask him. I'm not even sure it was drugs. All I know is he qualified as a police dog and it looked like he was alerting the way they get trained to.'

Terrance pursed his lips. It did look like the dog alerted. It could mean there were drugs inside the building right now. He would have to report it, but already knew they would tell him to sit tight. The minnow they had him watching wasn't big enough but if they had product on the premises, they would have to move it and that might reveal their distribution method.

'You're ex-police?' asked Silvio.

Albert nodded. 'Full career. Left on pension as a detective superintendent.'

Silvio was fairly sure the old man would say yes, which was why he asked him. Albert in turn, knew why the man asked. Silvio said, 'Then you'll know the importance of discretion.' He made eye contact with the girl as well to make sure she understood too. 'This cannot appear on social media ten minutes from now. It will blow the whole case. You understand, I am certain, just how hard it can be to build a case.'

Albert nodded. 'You can rely on us, officer.'

The matter with the police was dealt with, Albert giving Rex's lead a quick tug to get him moving again. His watch told him it was just after five. When he glanced back at the workshop, the roller door was down to signal the business was closed for the day. His hips and knees were becoming insistent that he take a break.

'I'm heading back to my B&B to rest,' he told Donna. 'I need to think about what we do next?'

'What can we do?' asked Donna, choosing to walk with Albert because his B&B was on the way to the hospital and evening visiting hours would start soon. Mum had told her not to bother; she was only going to be in for a couple of days, but it was too quiet at home without her and with work closed she wanted to update her on what had happened today.

'Well,' Albert started. 'Your business will not be able to reopen until the health ministry certify it as safe, which will take longer if there is an open case hanging over it. Until they analyse the meat taken from your shop to prove it isn't Mark Whitehouse,' Donna made a gagging face, 'they won't move the investigation on. If the disappearance of Mark

Whitehouse is connected to the drug investigation - I assume that is what we just stumbled across - then it may be months before they solve it. If they ever do.'

'They won't keep us closed for months though, surely?'

'No. But they won't be in a hurry to do anything to expedite it either. They have bigger issues to focus on. I had hoped we might determine what happened and maybe solve the case ourselves. That looks unlikely now, so I will contact my son, he's a detective superintendent in Kent, to see if he can pull a few strings to get your place cleared.'

'You'll do that?' Donna couldn't keep the relief from her voice.

'I can't promise anything,' Albert wanted to make clear. 'But I've come this far so I might as well see if I can get your place reopened before I go.'

'That's so generous of you. You've been nothing but generous since I brought the refund to the B&B.'

Albert didn't know what to say. His cheeks felt a little warm; he wasn't used to being praised. He changed the subject. 'Isn't your home in the other direction?'

'I'm on my way to the hospital to see mum.'

Accepting her reason, and glad it wasn't because she felt he might not find his way by himself, he soon turned into the short driveway of Mrs Worsley's bed and breakfast. 'This is me then. I'll let you know how I get on and call you later either way.'

Donna thanked him and waved goodbye, giving the dog a pat on the head as she left.

Neither looked across the street, but if they had, they most likely wouldn't have seen the pair of eyes looking at them over the top of a magazine.

'You look like an idiot,' said Mikey.

'Nonsense,' argued Malcolm. 'My disguise makes me invisible. I just look like a man reading a magazine. Whereas you look like a stalker.'

Mikey shook his head. 'You've walked into three trees, trodden in dog poop and fallen over two broken paving slabs. Not only that, you're holding a copy of Woman's World. You look like a berk.'

'And you're wearing dark sunglasses, a stupid hat, and you've got your collar turned up to hide as much of your ugly mug as possible. People will be thankful for the last part of that, but you look like a bad version of a bad guy from a Mickey Spillane novel.'

'No, I don't,' snarled Mikey. 'I look cool and dangerous. That's not an easy combination to pull off. You wouldn't know about that because you are neither.'

'Hey, where'd they go?' asked Malcolm.

Now feeling triumphant because he had been watching while Malcolm got distracted, Mikey replied, 'The old man went into that B&B with his big dog. The girl carried on. I expect she'll be back later.'

'Why?'

'Malcolm you really are dumb, you know that. She's about sixteen, right? So that's got to be her grandfather. That or a sugar daddy, but since I don't see him twirling a Bentley key and he's staying in a bed and breakfast and not the Ritz, I think we can rule out the latter. They'll be staying together.'

'What do we do now then?' asked Malcolm.

Glad to be in charge since Malcolm was asking all the questions, Mikey said, 'We get a fish 'n' chip supper, go shopping, and come back later.'

'What are we shopping for?'

'Interesting things, Malcolm. Interesting things.'

Bath Time

The screech came from behind, making him jump just as he placed his hand on the door handle to his room. Hoping his heart would restart shortly, Albert turned to find Mrs Worsley ten feet behind him with her hands clamped to her face.

He didn't have to ask what caused the look of horror currently displayed on her face; the line of oily dog prints was clear for anyone to see.

Albert said, 'Ah.'

'This is a wool carpet!' Mrs Worsley exclaimed. 'I'll have to get it professionally cleaned.' Her hands were still stuck to her head as if glued there, her eyes wide as she gawped at the line of prints on her cream carpet.

Albert wanted to point out that while it looked nice, cream wasn't the most practical colour for a bed and breakfast where foot traffic would be considerably higher than someone's house. He refrained though, choosing instead to examine Rex for more dirt.

He was covered. With an exasperated breath, he accepted his fate. 'It looks like you need a bath, old boy.'

For a moment, Rex thought his human was talking to himself. He did that quite often, Rex noticed. When he glanced upward, he realised the comment was aimed at him. 'Oh, no, you don't,' growled Rex, backing up.

Mrs Worsley screeched some more. 'He's grinding it in now. Pick him up quickly, pick him up.'

'He weighs more than me,' Albert chuckled, opening the door to his room. The carpet in there was the same cream colour which presented yet another problem. The dog had to get from where he was to the bathroom without touching the floor. Best to deal with the near-hysterical woman first. 'Mrs Worsley, please arrange to have the carpets cleaned and send me the bill.'

'Send you the bill?'' she echoed. 'Of course I'm going to send you the bill.' Her face was like a thundercloud. Stomping back down the stairs to make a phone call, her grumbling voice reached Albert's ears.

Albert let her go, accepted the bill in his head and considered his latest problem. 'Stay there, Rex.' He looped the lead over the door handle and crossed the room to the small suitcase lying open on top of the chest of drawers by the window. It was a bay window at the front of the house overlooking the street outside. If he had chosen to look, he might have seen two men across the street scanning the windows for signs of life, but in his hurry, he grabbed two pairs of socks and darted back to the dirty dog.

'I'm just going to slip these over your feet, Rex,' he explained as he slowly lowered himself to the carpet with a comment, 'Goodness, I'm sure it wasn't this far to the floor when I was younger.' He decided sitting was easiest, spreading out his legs as he grabbed the first paw, a back one, to put a sock on.

Getting up again was just as hard as getting down but now the dog, who bore a distinctly surly expression, had a sock on each foot. Albert didn't know if the socks would be salvageable after this, but at least he wouldn't wreck another carpet.

'I am not getting in the bath,' Rex assured him as Albert tried to coax him into the bathroom. 'I would rather try using your toilet, which, for the record, is disgusting. Why can't humans go outside like all other creatures?'

95

'Come on, Rex. Work with me,' Albert begged. The dog didn't want to budge, and he really did weigh more. If the dog wouldn't get into the bath, he wasn't sure how he was going to get him clean. 'I bet you'd go in a lake to chase a duck.'

'That's different,' growled Rex.

Several more exasperated breaths and some inventive swearwords later, Albert sat on the edge of the bath. 'I concede,' he said rather breathlessly, 'that a new approach might be called for.'

Rex didn't know what all the fuss was about. He just needed a good walk around the park, that would get the grime and stink off his paws, and a good roll in the dirt would not only make his coat feel better but would get the blobs of oil out of it too. His human seemed to have got the message, finally; he'd left the bathroom and was digging around in his suitcase.

Rex's ears pricked up the moment he heard Albert's hand close around the packet of gravy bones. He licked his lips and got to his feet. 'I am a good boy. You know I am. Bring that gravy bone over here, old man, and I might forget about the incident with Mitzy.

Albert waved the gravy bones back and forth in front of the dog's face, watching Rex's eyes follow it like he was tracking a metronome. He waited until Rex started to salivate, and his hind quarters twitched, then he threw it underarm over the dog's head.

Rex couldn't move his feet fast enough with the stupid socks on. The gravy bone was going to get away! Digging in with the claws of his back feet, he found purchase through the socks and leapt, catching it in mid-air just as he landed.

In the bath.

The bathroom door slammed shut behind him with the resounding clang of a death toll.

'Look before you leap,' chuckled Albert, turning on the tap and emptying a shampoo bottle onto the dog's shoulders. 'I think that might be my new favourite proverb.'

Rex crunched the gravy bone as the suds began to foam around his ears. The human thought he had won but this was just an early skirmish in the war to come. 'My revenge,' Rex assured him as he swallowed the gravy bone, 'will be as silent as it will be inescapable.'

Albert ran a bath for himself once the dog was clean. The towels were hopelessly soaked, all bar a small hand towel barely a foot square, but he could drip dry if necessary. While the tub filled and the dog sulked, Albert's phone rang.

It was Randall. 'Hello, Randall.'

'Hi, dad,' his youngest replied. 'Sorry. I meant to get back to you sooner but got caught up with things here. It cost me a favour I might not enjoy repaying, but I have the forensic analysis for the thumb.'

'Oh, yes?'

'It had been somewhere near a mechanic's place, breaker's yard, or car repair centre of some kind. That was the conclusion they drew. The skin was embedded with tiny particles of carbon saturated oil, the kind you get out of an engine when the oil needs changing. Also, gasoline and tiny particles of different metals, all commonly found around mechanics.'

'I was there earlier,' Albert pursed his lips in thought.

'You were there? You were where someone had their thumb torn off? What are you up to, dad?' Randall sounded both upset and worried.

Albert sighed. 'I'm just helping someone out. It's not a big deal. No one is taking any notice of me. Please stop worrying and tell your siblings to do the same.'

'Are you sure, dad? Wouldn't you rather come home?'

'Quite sure, son.' Randall's attitude was disappointing. Albert thought his youngest was behind him setting off to explore while he still could. His change in attitude meant Gary had got to him. Albert thought himself clever when he called different children to get bits of information, Selina was next on his list, but they were obviously talking to one another. 'I'm not coming home any time soon, Randall. When you talk to Gary and Selina next, you can tell them that too.'

They said goodnight and Albert went to get in his bath. His kids acted as if he was going to stir up trouble and get into a gun battle with mobsters or something. He gave his reflection a wry smile as he slipped his clothes off.

He might not have done had he known what was to come.

Brenda had been in a bad mood for the last two days. Her perfect, slick little operation, her demonstration of ingenuity, had gone horribly wrong because of one man's greed and now she was going to have to shut the whole thing down.

Worse yet was the need to explain it to her boss. He would find out anyway, which meant it was in her best interest to get ahead of the information and deliver it to him in a way that gave it a positive spin.

Reluctantly, and with an exhaled breath of annoyance, she made the call.

'Brenda. Are you calling to admit that my operation has fallen foul of your bad management?'

Dammit he already knew! It would have been Mikey or Malcolm. They were the boss's cousins and loyal to him first. She didn't miss his goading choice of words either: his operation, her bad management.

Through tight lips, she replied, 'It was nothing more than bad luck. Manufacture can continue while I look for a new distribution hub. Impact to supply will be minimal and I plan to make a double batch tomorrow night to make up for the two missed days.'

At the other end, the man stayed silent. He liked using silence as a tactic because it made people uncomfortable; sooner or later, they always felt the need to fill the void. Brenda was no different.

'I need better men to work with,' she complained, which he felt was an admission of guilt.

Asserting his dominance, he pushed her into a corner. 'You feel my family members are not pulling their weight?'

She wanted to reply that they were both incompetent idiots. It wasn't wise to insult a man she knew to be responsible for dozens of deaths, so she bit her tongue instead. She chose her words carefully. 'I ... they look to me for constant guidance. I am used to working with those who can operate autonomously.'

'Very well. You plan to evacuate the distribution facility and clean house?' He didn't like Brenda and had thought about killing her several times in the past. She was a capable operator but not one he trusted.

'Yes.'

'What is your timeline?'

'I have everything geared to shut down after production tomorrow night. We'll use the stocked product we have here. Manufacture will be cleared out tomorrow morning and the distribution hub that night. All the buildings will be destroyed, and all the loose ends eliminated.'

'What will you do with the bodies?' he asked.

A small snort of laughter escaped her lips. 'I have an excellent method of disposal. Believe me when I say they will never be found.'

'Excellent,' the boss said. Finally, Brenda felt she could breathe a sigh of relief. He had accepted the changes to the plan – something he was famous for refusing to tolerate – and she could get on with it uninterrupted. 'I'll supervise in person. Ensure everything is ready for my arrival.'

'There's really no need,' she blurted. The last thing in the world she wanted was him looking over her shoulder.

'Oh? You think to know what is best for my operation, do you?'

'No, I ...'

'I'll be there at eight.'

Brenda didn't get a chance to argue, he hung the phone up as soon as the threat was delivered. She glared at her phone accusingly and thought about throwing it at the wall. He would find something to complain about, levy blame on her for some minor imperfection. Her operation ran smoothly for five months and might have continued were it not for Mark Whitehouse.

Sleeping Soundly

It was an unfortunate truth of his age, that Albert could not get through the night without having to get up and pee. He couldn't remember when it started but it was some time ago now. This was the first time tonight, but he usually got up more than once.

The small bedside clock claimed the time to be just before midnight; the earliness of his first nocturnal interruption increasing the likelihood that there would be another. Rex was sleeping in the corner of the room where Albert banished him after he got under the bed and farted continuously for an hour. He needed to threaten him with castration just to get him to move and neither was talking to the other currently.

'Nobody light a match,' he grumbled as he shut the bathroom door and turned on the light.

Before he could loosen the drawstring on his pyjama bottoms, a smashing noise startled him. Rex barked instantly but it was the whump of ignition that gripped Albert's attention to cause a rush of adrenalin.

Ripping the door open revealed an inferno on the other side. 'Rex!' Albert shouted, knowing he had seconds to get out or fight the fire. His bedsheets were ablaze and already threatening to set fire to the headboard. It would take no time for the flames to spread to everything in the room and suck out all the oxygen. It would be over a thousand degrees in seconds.

A fire alarm burst into life, so loud it almost defied belief at a time when all his other senses were being assailed. Struggling against the heat, Albert shielded his eyes and shouted again, 'Rex!' There was no sign of him. Would his still soggy fur give him the seconds he needed to get out when Albert opened the door?

Still soggy!

Albert remembered the terrible mess he made of the towels trying to get Rex dry and then the fight they had with the hairdryer. Fast as he could, Albert ducked back into the bathroom and grabbed the bundle of towels from the bath. He didn't have the hand strength to wring them out anymore, so they were still sodden.

Remembering the technique to put out a fire in a chip pan, he held a bath sheet in front of his face with his hands fully extended above his head, held his breath and laid it over the bed.

The fire there went out almost instantly though there were flames licking at the carpet and on the nightstand where the flammable liquid had splashed. Albert stamped on the carpet and grabbed another towel.

The door burst open, his shouts alerting and alarming other guests and Mrs Worsley who appeared in the doorway a few seconds later. Mrs Worsley's horrified wails of anguish filled the air and the shouts from terrified guests wondering what had happened threatened to bubble over into a panic. People were running past his door to get outside even as a man in just his underwear fought through the smoke to get into the room.

The fire was out, but Albert couldn't stop coughing. He caught a lungful of the awful smoke when he couldn't hold his breath any longer, but his concern was for Rex. He tried to shout for him again, but just coughed more instead.

Hands tried to help him from his destroyed room, but he fought them, needing to know where his dog was.

'He's got a dog!' exclaimed Mrs Worsley, thankfully more concerned for preservation of life, than for the Egyptian cotton towels he used to extinguish the fire.

The man in his boxer shorts got on his knees and called for the dog. Not knowing his name, he shouted, 'Here, boy!' The light was on, but the room was so filled with smoke, it was almost impossible to see.

Albert staggered into the hallway outside, still coughing, but managed to blurt, 'Rex. His name's Rex.'

When the shout came between coughs that he had found him, Albert felt his heart soar. The man appeared through the smoke with Rex held against his chest as he carried the large dog out of the smoke-filled room.

As the sound of sirens grew in volume, Albert and Rex huddled on the carpet. It still bore Rex's paw prints but that was of little concern now compared to the mess of Albert's room. 'I think we stepped on someone's toes, Rex,' said Albert. He checked the dog over for burns but there were none. His fur had a slightly smoky scent to it but mostly it still smelled like shampoo. So close to the floor, Rex managed to escape smoke inhalation, escaping the burning room unscathed.

He gave his human a lick. 'Maybe you're not so bad,' Rex conceded. 'I heard you calling for me and you did put out the fire. Your nose might not work properly, but you do your best to make up for it with other skills.'

'Are you alright?' asked the man in his boxer shorts. He was in his late twenties and athletic-looking in a way that Albert had been at that age.

'I'm fine, thank you,' Rex answered, only realising afterward that the man was addressing his human.

'Just got a lungful of that smoke,' Albert replied, playing it down. 'I'll be fine. I'm not burned, and the dog is okay. Thank you for getting him.'

A young woman, the man's wife presumably, had her hand on the man's shoulder as he crouched to check on Albert. 'The fire brigade are here,' she told them both.

Mrs Worsley continued to wail, the event too much for her to be able to take in. The young couple, satisfied Albert was alright, set about guiding her outside. The fire might be out, but the house was filled with smoke. Albert pushed off the carpet, and with Rex sticking close to his side, he made his way down the stairs and outside into the cool autumn air.

The paramedics insisted Albert have oxygen when they arrived, escorting him to the ambulance outside in the street so they could check his vitals and monitor him. They wanted to take him to hospital for further observation, but he wouldn't hear of it.

Everyone inside evacuated outside, a dozen guests, all in their nightwear or whatever they managed to grab on their way out. They wanted to get back inside where it was warm and couldn't understand why the firefighters barred their entry if the fire was already out.

The lead firefighter entertained no discussion on the subject. The mattress, which caught most of the fuel, was carried outside where Albert got to see just how lucky he had been. His weak bladder saved his life.

It was arson; not that Albert had any doubt, but the lead firefighter confirmed it upon removing the towel and inspecting the bed. A petrol bomb: a crude glass jar that once held jam, had been attached to a rock, lit, and then tossed through his window. Maybe it was a lucky shot, maybe they knew exactly where the bed was in that room. One thing was for sure in Albert's mind: he had been the target.

'What makes you say that?' asked a police officer, a sergeant called Buchanan. The police showed up because everyone else was already there, but the declaration of arson got them interested.

'I need you to find a young girl called Donna Agnew,' announced Albert. He'd had enough of being monitored. The cough would stay with him for a few days he expected, but it wasn't enough to stop him getting up when a sudden thought crossed his mind – if they came after him, they could easily go after her as well.

Ignoring the paramedics repeated pleas to take him to hospital, Albert climbed down from the ambulance and sidestepped the police officer. He needed his phone, that was the fastest way to check if she was alright.

His path was immediately blocked by another man who then thrust a microphone in his face as the man on his shoulder took pictures. 'Tragedy averted at second rate doss house. Tell us about your ordeal, sir.'

It was that terrible hack reporter Peterson again. Albert tried to sidestep him. 'No comment.'

Peterson didn't even blink and certainly didn't get out of the way, walking backwards with his microphone held under Albert's face. 'What can you tell us about the fire, sir? Was it substandard electrics that caused it?'

Mrs Worsley heard his question. 'Substandard what? Who said my electrics are substandard?' Peterson swung toward the sound of her voice and started heading her way.

From the corner of his eye, Albert saw the lead firefighter signal something and suddenly one of the hoses leapt into life. He had to guess that Peterson was well known in the town, for less than halfway to Mrs Worsley a jet of water smacked him in the side of his head.

'Donna who?' asked Sergeant Buchanan, walking fast to keep up with the old man now that the reporter issue was dealt with.

Heading for the door to go back inside, Albert was thinking fast. 'Hey!' He waved to the lead firefighter, a man in his early forties with salt and pepper hair showing beneath his helmet. 'Have there been any other attacks like this one tonight? Or any fires at all?' he asked when the man looked his way.

Wondering why the question was asked, he answered anyway, 'There was one fire but it was at a commercial unit, not a house. Why?'

'Because there might be,' Albert's response came out dripping with the dread such a statement warranted. Turning his head to look at the police sergeant, he said, 'I need to speak with Detective Sergeant Moss too.'

At the door to the house a firefighter moved to intercept him. 'You can't go back in yet, sir.'

'I need my phone! The arsonist might be planning another attack tonight.' Albert expected this; all the other residents were still stuck outside while the police and fire brigade went over the house to make sure it was all safe. 'If we don't warn them, the next target might not be so lucky.'

Albert could see the indecision on the man's face, but he didn't have to press any further, Sergeant Buchanan stepped in. 'Tell me where your phone is. I'll get it.'

Sixty seconds later, he pressed the button to connect to Donna's phone. It rang and rang. Albert had Sergeant Buchanan listening in, plus a couple of the firefighters who were keen to find out if there really was a serial arsonist about.

When the call switched over to voicemail, Sergeant Buchanan asked, 'Where does she live? I can get a car to do a drive by.'

Albert grimaced. 'I don't know. I only met her yesterday morning.' Then he quickly explained how they met and why he thought she might be in trouble.

'And that's why you want to speak to Moss,' the sergeant concluded. 'Okay, I think we can track her down. Her mum is the owner of Agnew's Perfect Pork Pie Emporium?' He was talking to himself as he unclipped his radio, relaying the details to a voice at the other end. He waited with the radio held near his face for an answer to come back, less than a minute elapsing before the address came through.

'Do you want me to send a car?' asked the voice in dispatch.

Sergeant Buchanan shook his head even though the person in dispatch couldn't see it. 'No, I'll go myself. It might be nothing.'

When he went inside, Albert begged the sergeant to grab his suitcase; the phone was next to it. He complied but looked surprised now that the old man was putting clothes on over his pyjamas. 'I need to see for myself,' Albert explained.

With an arm around Rex as he laid across the back seats and Albert's lap, Albert looked out the window and tried to settle his stomach. He felt sick with worry for the young girl as the police car raced across town with its blue lights flashing. He pressed dial again and held the phone to his ear but got the same result as the previous ten attempts.

Mercifully, in a car breaking the speed limit, the journey didn't take long. Sergeant Buchanan was good enough to call out the streets as they went, telling Albert how close they were as they all peered out the windows for signs of smoke or fire. There were none.

As they swung into her street, it became obvious Albert's concerns were a false alarm; there were no flames licking from the windows of any house and most especially not the one the squad car stopped in front of.

Sergeant Buchanan unclipped his seat belt. 'Stay here, I'll knock.' Albert thought the message was more for his driver's ears than his, but he stayed put and watched through the window, holding his breath until a light came on in an upstairs window.

Moments later, the outside light turned on to illuminate the police officer before the door opened a crack. Albert couldn't see Donna, but the relaxed posture of Sergeant Buchanan allowed him to relax in turn.

Rex sensed the change in his human. The old man had been tense ever since the fire in their room. Rex tried to calm him by staying close, but something changed in the last second. Popping his head up, he saw the girl who'd been with them the last couple of days. Recognising her, he wagged his tail.

'You want to see her, boy?' asked Albert, opening the car door.

Donna had awoken to an insistent hammering. Instantly scared in her groggy state, it took her a few seconds to understand what the person at her door was shouting. What the heck did the police want at this time of the night?

The police officer on her doorstep was telling her something - or trying to. She was having trouble making out what he said around a yawn that split her face in two. Then suddenly, a huge dog came bounding out of the dark. Her adrenalin kicked in a split second before she spotted Albert's face in the back of the police car and worked out the dog was Rex.

Rex didn't bother to stop when he got to the house. It was a house and that meant it would have a kitchen. He wasn't used to being up at this time of day and all the activity and excitement had made him hungry.

Seeing his dog shoot straight into the house, Albert muttered a word his wife would have told him off for using and clambered out to fetch him. He continued muttering all the way up the short drive to the step Sergeant Buchanan still occupied.

'Good morning, Donna. Sorry about waking you.'

'That's okay, Albert. The police officer explained what happened at the B&B. Are you and Rex alright?' Donna yawned again. She had on a thigh-length nightshirt with a picture of a sleepy bunny holding a cup of cocoa. It wasn't doing much to ward off the cold and she had her arms wrapped around her middle.

'We're both fine,' Albert assured her. 'Rex is for sure. Shall I get him, or do you want to chase him out?'

'Where are you going to stay now?' Donna asked. 'It's the middle of the night. Come inside and crash on the spare bed. Mum wouldn't hear of me letting you go elsewhere.' When he hesitated, Donna insisted, 'Get inside, Albert, I'm getting cold.'

Albert looked at Sergeant Buchanan who just shrugged. 'I guess you don't need me anymore. I'll pass that message along to DS Moss and let her know where to find you. I expect she'll call when she comes on shift in the morning.'

Albert thanked the man, and shuffled inside, passing Donna as she held the door open and closed it behind him. Rex bounded back out from wherever he had been to land at his feet. His tongue lolled out and he clearly wanted to play.

Donna yawned again. 'We should let you get to bed,' Albert said, feeling bad again that he had woken her.

Donna tried to stifle the yawn, grabbing the wall for support until it passed by itself. 'Wow. Goodness. I think we should all get to bed. You're sure you are alright?'

'I'm fine. It's Mrs Worsley the landlady I feel sorry for and all the other guests.'

Donna pursed her lips. 'You think this was because we went to the repair yard, don't you?'

Albert had to nod. 'I do. You're right about the sleep, though,' he managed as a yawn split his face too.

Inspired to join in, Rex also yawned. There didn't seem to be any food on offer, so sleep was his next choice.

Breakfast Guests

Albert awoke in a confused state and a wall in front of his eyes that ought not to be there. It took only a moment for his brain to catch up, but those first few seconds of alertness caught him by surprise until the previous evening's events flooded back.

Ironically, the few hours he snatched on Donna's mum's spare bed, a single tucked into the smallest room in the house, were the best of his trip so far. The smell of bacon assailed his nostrils when he sat up and shuffled around to get his legs pointing the right way. The smell also explained the absence of his dog, who was no doubt very close to the scent's origin.

Half of his things were still at Mrs Worsley's bed and breakfast; he would need to return to collect them, sort out paying for the carpet to be cleaned and apologise for the terrible mess. Not that he felt responsible; he hadn't thrown the petrol bomb, but it was also true that had he not stayed there, Mrs Worsley would have avoided all the trouble his presence brought.

Thankfully, his suitcase contained enough clean clothes to make up a fresh outfit for the day which he hung up as he dug around to find his toiletry bag. Shuffling to the bathroom, he heard voices downstairs, both male and female which he discovered, some ten minutes later, belonged to Donna, obviously, DS Moss and DC Wright.

They all turned as he entered the room, Rex getting up to greet his human.

DS Moss slid off her stool at the breakfast bar to greet him. 'Good morning, Mr Smith. It appears you ignored my advice and attracted the interest of unknown parties who did not wish to have you prying into their business.' She was berating him but in a good-natured way; she saw little to be gained from shouting at an old man.

'Would you like some breakfast?' asked Donna. 'I can do you a full English. I've got all the trimmings.'

Feeling his attention split, Albert nevertheless eyed the counter with interest. 'Do you have any black pudding?'

Donna held up a long black-skinned sausage. 'I even have kidneys.' His stomach growled at the suggestion, and Rex jumped up to balance on his back feet briefly because all the food smells and talk were too much. 'Oh, I haven't fed Rex yet,' Donna added upon seeing the dog. 'He has been asking for an hour, but I don't have any dog food in and wasn't sure what you might want to let him have.'

It was a day for there to be treats, Albert decided. 'He can have a full English too, if that's alright with you.'

Rex spun on the spot.

Donna got started on making another pair of breakfast plates, but DS Moss wanted to get down to business. 'I got to the station this morning to find an instruction to find you. I'm guessing you have something you want to tell me?'

'Is there any tea?' asked Albert, looking about for a pot.

Donna reached out with one hand to flick a button and press the kettle into service. He really wanted a cup of tea to wake himself up properly, but DS Moss had been good enough to come to Donna's house and then waited patiently for him to rise, so it was only fair he answered her question promptly.

113

'We ran into a dead end, Detective Sergeant. I'm sure you saw the CCTV camera footage showing Mark Whitehouse coming into the rear of the pork pie emporium's property by climbing over a wall. An impressive feat with one hand. That led us to an auto-repair centre in the street behind.'

'Blake's,' DS Moss supplied.

Albert nodded. 'I believe he received his injury there and escaped. I also believe the business is a front for something else.' DS Moss looked at him quizzically. 'We found the cops staking it out,' he explained.

DS Moss knew of the operation, she stumbled across it herself as soon as she watched the CCTV footage and started digging into the businesses tucked behind the pork pie shop. She got firmly told to stop investigating. 'I know about the operation,' she replied guardedly.

'Then you will know the thumb got into the pork pie meat supply by accident and Mark Whitehouse wasn't part of the pies being served that day.'

'Actually, I don't. Mark Whitehouse still hasn't been located. The last sighting is on the CCTV footage taken by the camera on the rear of Agnew's Perfect Pork Pie Emporium. His whereabouts are still unknown.'

A little exasperated, Albert flapped his arms. 'But surely you are testing the meat to prove it is pork and not human?'

Not used to being quizzed, DS Moss narrowed her eyes when she replied. 'That task is underway but may take some time. It was only two days ago that the thumb was found, Mr Smith. A little patience is required with police work. You, of all people, ought to understand that.'

He bit down any retort because he knew she was right. Instead, he changed tack slightly. 'The family need to reopen their shop.'

'I am sure they do,' DS Moss expected this to be the key driver behind his request to see her. 'My boss received a request from an old friend, a detective superintendent called Gary Smith. He wouldn't have to be a relative, would he, Mr Smith?'

'My son,' Albert admitted.

DS Moss came a step closer. 'I do not appreciate being summoned, Mr Smith. I especially do not like it when my boss calls me into his office to ask me if I am dragging my feet. I cannot solve the case of Mark Whitehouse's disappearance without tripping over a national investigation which takes priority. Sticking my nose into it would be tantamount to career suicide. That means the forensic team must go through every piece of meat to be certain it is not a piece of Mark Whitehouse and until that task is complete, I will not be able to categorically state to the health ministry that Agnew's Perfect Pork Pie Emporium did not serve human flesh to their customers. Only then, will they conduct their own inspection and determine whether the shop can reopen.'

'That's hardly fair,' Donna complained.

'Life's like that,' replied DS Moss, her eyes firmly fixed on Albert's. 'I could wish it were different but wishing will not get us anywhere. If you want to get your shop open sooner, find out who's behind the drug trade and how they are shipping it around the country. All I know is that they have been trying to catch this firm for a year and hit nothing but dead ends. Quite why they think a major drug operation is centred in Melton Mowbray I cannot imagine.' Message delivered, DS Moss saw no reason to waste any more of her day. She and Wright were reassigned to a different case the moment she triggered the national drug squad's radar and it was time to get on with it.

Albert followed them to the door so Donna could continue cooking. At the door, he said, 'Thank you for coming in person Detective Sergeant. Could I have a direct dial number for you?'

'Why would you want that? Didn't you tell me two days ago that you were on a tour of Great Britain and about to move on?'

'I did. I did say that, and I will be moving on just as soon as I have done as you suggested.' DS Moss gave him a blank look. 'Work out who's behind the drug trade and how they are shipping it around the country. That was the suggestion you made. I'll get that done, call you to arrest everyone and then, once Donna's shop is open again, I'll make my perfect pork pie and be on my merry way.'

DS Moss had her mouth hanging open. The old man just didn't know when to quit. 'I was being flippant,' she growled. 'You are to stay away from Blake's Auto Repairs and away from anything to do with the disappearance of Mark Whitehouse.' Her instruction could not be clearer.

Albert gave her his innocent face, 'Of course. I would never dream of interfering.'

'Good. I'm glad we understand each other.'

'I'll be investigating the appearance of a thumb in Donna's shop. That's a whole different thing.'

DS Moss's face changed gear, going directly from bored to rage, but the front door swung shut in her face as the old man closed it.

Albert hadn't wanted to be rude, but crimes were never solved like this in his day, and yet they got solved. Someone tried to firebomb him into an early grave last night; not very early admittedly, but early, nevertheless. They endangered his dog too and he felt some payback was due, even if just so Mrs Worsley could name the people who trashed his room.

Feeling a sense of purpose he recognised, but hadn't possessed for more than two decades, Albert knew what he needed to do next.

He needed to eat breakfast!

Wholesale

In truth, Albert didn't know how he was going to solve the crime and get Donna's shop reopened. Her mum was coming out of hospital the following morning, something Donna was very thankful for, but he wished she had better news.

When Donna visited her in hospital last night, she found her mum to be quite stoical about their situation; at least that was how Donna made it sound to Albert. They had customers and they had staff and they had a good kitchen in their house, so they were just going to have to get back to basics and make the best with what they had. Her mum didn't want to wait another day to get started so Donna called the two guys who cut the meat and prepared the pies, and the two women who baked and presented them. With both Donna and her mum on speakerphone, they convinced each of them to come to her house after lunch. They were going to get the business back into production. It was that or risk their main customers having to go elsewhere for their supply.

Walk-in customers who came in the shop were ninety percent tourists passing by and not repeat customers, so the focus had to be on the local shops, restaurants and pubs who bought dozens or even hundreds at a time.

Donna's big task for the morning was to buy ingredients from the wholesalers. A call to their usual butcher reduced the size of the order and diverted it to her house. It was coming at noon. Everything else she could get under one roof, but she had to go there to get it.

'You can drive, right?' said Donna, handing Albert the keys to her mum's van.

He looked at the bunch in his right hand with wide eyes. 'Um, in theory.' It had been years since he got behind the wheel. He still had a driver's licence because he hadn't seen the need to relinquish it. Now it was going to bite him on the bum.

'Well, I can't drive. I'm sixteen.'

'Right. Okay then.' Albert wondered if this was a good idea, especially when he saw the size of the Ford Transit van he needed to drive. 'Perhaps we should get one of the staff to drive it,' he suggested.

'No time,' said Donna, pulling an oops face. 'They won't get here until after noon and we have a slot at the wholesalers for ten o'clock. If we miss it, we won't get in again until tomorrow. We have to go now. Sorry, I just assumed you could drive.'

'Like riding a bike,' he muttered as he opened the driver's door.

Rex rode between them both, Donna's arm around his waist to hold him in place. Not that she thought it was necessary, glancing at the speedo to check they were still only doing twenty-five miles per hour.

'Everything okay?' Albert enquired, his voice like honey when he saw her looking at the speedometer. *Yes, I'm going slow so we get there alive, put up with it.*

'Nothing, Albert. Nothing at all,' she grinned back at him. 'We just got overtaken by a man walking his poodle.'

'You can get out and run if you prefer. I'll meet you there.'

'You don't know where you are going,' she chuckled, wondering if running might actually be quicker. Seriously concerned that she might miss her slot, they cruised into the carpark just in time, but she got a nasty shock when she saw who was going through the doors right ahead of them.

Hearing her mutter, Albert asked, 'Something the matter?'

Donna had an angry expression, her face screwed up as she squinted to the distance. 'That's Toby Simmons.'

Albert spotted the Simmons van with its colourful livery and tasty looking pork pie emblazoned on the side beneath the legend, "Melton Mowbray's Best".

'Do you know how they got away with that sign?' Donna asked, seeing where Albert was looking. 'It doesn't say best what. Mum lost a pile of money hiring a lawyer to make them take that down. He promised us he would win and then said it was just one of those things when he lost.'

'Then he wanted you to settle his bill in full, didn't he?'

'Yup. Every penny. Those Simmons have a lot to answer for.' Donna bumped the door open with her hip, putting a hand out to stop Rex from following her. 'You have to stay here, boy.'

Rex raised one eyebrow. 'I'm an assistance dog. It says so on the side of my jacket. I get to go everywhere.' When she closed the door, he spun around to go the other way.

'Sorry, Rex,' said Albert. Not this time. I won't be long. You guard the van.' Then, because they had collected all his things from Mrs Worsley's on their way to the wholesalers, he fished into his bag to find the dog chews and handed Rex one to appease him.

'Yeah,' said Rex with the chew sticking out of his mouth. 'I'll guard the van. Nobody's gonna steal the van with me in it.' He didn't bother to watch his human go; the chew deserved his full attention.

120

At the wholesaler, Donna checked in, grabbed one of the big catering trolleys and peered cautiously up the first aisle.

'Do you know where everything is?' asked a helpful assistant.

Donna straightened herself. 'Yes, thank you. I'm trying to avoid someone who is already in the shop,' she explained, then spotted Toby coming out of an aisle ahead of her. Before he could turn his head her way, she zipped up the first aisle she came to.

Albert rolled his eyes and shuffled after her. Two aisles over she started to pull plain flour from a pallet on the floor. Grunting with each fifty-pound sack, she took six of them and had them loaded before Albert caught up.

'That's the heavy bit,' she told him. 'Now we need lard and milk and about two hundred eggs, plus celery, carrots, and onions, plus spices and herbs.' She rolled her eyes to the top of her skull as she went through her mental checklist. 'Yeah, that's it.'

'I didn't know there were carrots and other veggies in a pork pie,' remarked Albert with a frown. He'd only ever made one. It was at the Simmons' place yesterday and he didn't get to eat it, but there were no onions or carrots in it.

'They go in the gelatine that binds the meat inside the pastry. You didn't get to do that bit yesterday because it goes in when the pies come out of the oven. Pig's trotters and pork bones are the bit that makes it jellified; the butcher will deliver those along with the meat.'

They moved on, Donna stacking the trolley high with ingredients.

'Oi, wonky,' the insult was delivered with a sneer, the voice loud enough for most in the shop to hear as Toby Simmons approached them from behind.

Caught up in her shopping and thinking about the glorious afternoon of baking ahead, Donna had forgotten he was in the shop with them. She spun about on the spot, wanting very much to punch him in the face; there was no need for his malice. Her desire to hurt him stopped abruptly when she saw the two men standing in the queue to pay.

Toby, who had been ready to exchange insults and laugh about her shop going out of business, was suddenly faced with empty space as Donna grabbed the old man's arm and yanked him up an aisle.

Halfway through debating whether to give the boy a lesson in manners, or whether it was more politically correct these days to let the lady do it, Albert wasn't expecting the hard yank his left sleeve received and almost lost his balance.

'It's them,' squeaked Donna.

Not following, he asked, 'They who? It's the Simmons boy you wanted to avoid.'

She shook her head vigorously and peeked around the corner to check if they'd been spotted. She couldn't see them because Toby Simmons was in her way, leaning nonchalantly against the end of the aisle as he waited for her to pluck up the courage to respond.

She grabbed his shirt and yanked him around the corner too.

'Hey, mind the threads, wonky. With your mum's firm going bust, you won't have the money to buy me a new one.' He made a big show of straightening his shirt and brushing out the creases. He had a pair of men from his family shop with him, both in the family's livery. They were standing by two fully laden carts. He was the one with the store card and showing off because his dad owned the business. 'You go, guys. I'll catch up to you at the till.'

It was all he had time to say before Donna grabbed his groin and walked him backward to press him against the shelves. The two men from his family shop decided to hang around and watch for a bit, one taking out his phone to get some photographs. The kid might be one of the family, but his dad knew what was what and would laugh when they told him the tale later.

Hissing into his face as she squeezed, Donna said, 'Call me wonky one more time and I'll cut this thing off and turn it into a sausage roll.' She glanced down and back up with a menacing grin. 'A very small one.'

Toby attempted to move away, grabbing her wrist with both hands as he tried to prise her fingers open. Having learned from Rex, she squeezed a little harder. 'Ah!' Toby winced. 'Okay, no more name calling, you insane cow.'

Another squeeze. Toby's face was going white.

Albert sidled up next to him. 'It might be wise to apologise to the lady,' he suggested.

'Yes, yes, I'm sorry.'

Another squeeze made him jump on the spot. 'What's my name?'

'Donna,' he blurted. 'I'm sorry, Donna.'

The two Simmons staff nudged each other: this was good stuff.

Donna remembered why she was hiding in the first place and let Toby go. He sagged to his knees as she went back to look around the corner. They were still there.

Fun over, the Simmons men grabbed their trolleys and started toward the till area.

Donna tugged at Albert's sleeve, peering around the corner once more. Then, when he joined her, she pointed.

Albert saw it too. At the till, paying for their goods were the two men from Blake's Auto Repairs. They didn't know their names and they were dressed differently from yesterday, but it was unmistakably them.

'What are they doing here?' asked Donna, her voice a hushed whisper.

'Shopping.' Albert knew his reply wasn't helpful, but it was accurate. They *were* shopping, it was what they were buying that he wanted to know. 'We have to see what's in their carts.'

Just as soon as he said it, the two men from Simmons joined the back of the queue and completely blocked any chance they had of seeing what the mechanics were buying.

'What are you two doing?' asked Toby, recovered enough to stand and ask questions. Donna reached out to catch his arm but this time he darted away, too wise to get caught twice.

'I need your help,' she implored.

'You need my...' Toby's laugh came out deep and wholesome. It was fake, but he meant it. 'Wonk ... um, Donna, you have some nerve.'

'Why are you here anyway?' she asked, changing subject suddenly. 'You work in the shop, not in the factory.'

Toby shrugged. 'The factory manager, Adam Dodd, didn't show up for work the last two days. Dad and Uncle Don have had to put in extra hours to cover, and other than the factory manager, they're the only ones with catering cards. Dad said he needed me to come today. I've got to learn all the parts of running the business because it will be mine soon,' he bragged.

Albert wished to clarify a point. 'Your factory manager stopped coming to work the same night as your night watchman vanished and left his thumb across the street, yes? Do the police know?'

Toby thought about the question. 'Don't think so. They didn't ask dad anything like that. It's not the first time. He's gone on a bender before and taken a few days to sleep it off. Dad was pretty upset this time, though, I think he might just fire him when he resurfaces.'

'Young man we really do need your help. The two men currently paying for their goods.' He edged to the corner and pointed them out. 'I believe they are involved in a crime which led to Mark Whitehouse losing his thumb. I need to know what they are buying but they have met Donna and me so neither of us can get too close.'

'I'm not going over there if they are criminals!' Toby backed away. 'What if they pull a gun and rob the place. I could get killed in the crossfire.'

'Oh, grow a set will you, Toby,' snapped Donna.

'They are paying for their goods,' Albert pointed out. 'Not robbing the place. We just need you to go out to the carpark and have a look at what is in their cart as you pass them. They won't even notice you.'

Still not looking entirely sure about it, Toby blew out a breath through his nose and did as Albert asked. However, like a lot of people when they try to be inconspicuous, Toby stood out like a three-hundred-pound male rugby player in an under elevens ballet class. For girls.

He whistled loudly for a start, which made everyone look at him. Then, when the two men from Blake's Auto Repair looked at him, he coughed to clear his throat, turned scarlet, and started talking, 'Don't mind me. I'm just minding my own business. I'm not interested in anything anyone else is doing.'

'We're going to have to follow him,' said Donna.

'You still need to buy your goods.' No sooner had Albert said that, than a cashier took a seat behind a vacant register and started to open a new line. The guys from Blake's were going out the door. Toby was already outside, and they needed to hurry, so Donna seized her chance.

'I'm going for it,' she blurted, shoving her weight against the cart to get it moving. Surging forward, another woman in the queue ahead saw the new till open and started to switch lanes. Donna almost ran her over, their carts clanging off one another with a spark as Donna raced to get to the till first. She got an outraged shout of disgust, but Donna threw her loose goods to the cashier, and once they were being scanned, it was too late.

Albert went to the door to look outside. Toby was plastered against a van with his back pressed up tight against it as he craned his neck around the edge to look where the two mechanics were going. They had a plain white van in the far corner of the carpark. That they had parked so far away when the car park was only half full was suspicious, Albert thought, but then he knew they were up to no good anyway.

Donna raced out though the automatic doors, crouched down so the goods on her cart hid her face, but the men from Blake's were paying no attention to anything she was doing.

126

Albert walked up to Toby. 'Did you see what they bought?' he asked.

Toby screamed and almost collapsed.

Malcolm and Mikey both turned to see where the noise had come from, but all they saw was a cart seemingly making its way across the carpark by itself. They had too many other things to do and Brenda impatiently tapping her foot until they returned.

'Are you quite alright, young man?' Albert asked the form at his feet.

'No, I'm not! You scared the bejesus out of me!' He held a hand to his chest. 'Is seventeen too young to have a heart attack? I think I might be having one right now.'

Donna arrived with her cartful of flour, lard and sundries. 'You are such a drama queen, Toby Simmons. Get up and help me load this stuff, we have to follow them.'

'We? What's this 'we' nonsense?' Toby clambered off the floor, his heart attack now forgotten. 'I have to get back to the shop. Dad's expecting the ingredients. We ran inexplicably short when there ought to be plenty and Adam, the factory manager, isn't around to explain the discrepancy.'

Donna wasn't listening to his argument. 'Your family is in this whether you like it or not, Toby. It's not just my shop. It's yours too. Your night watchman and your factory manager go missing on the same day, one of them leaves his thumb behind and we know Mark Whitehouse was mixed up in something nefarious. Send your guys back to the shop; you need to come with us.'

'Why? What are you going to do?' Toby didn't look convinced, but he wasn't trying to walk away either.

The mechanics were almost done loading their van. If she didn't hurry up, they were going to miss them. Ripping open the side door, she said, 'Quick, just help me get these things in.'

Toby griped but grabbed a bag of flour because it was the fastest way to get her off his back. Load the van, then leave her here. The old man was packing the vegetables into the van and Donna was putting the caterers' packs of eggs, milk, and lard in, which left him to do the heavy work. He tugged his shirt sleeves up a bit to made sure she could see his biceps.

'Can you stack that one over the far side to even out the weight, please?' Donna asked. Toby swung his head around to offer her a frown because the task was completely unnecessary. There wasn't that much weight going in. But she smiled at him in a demure way and he remembered why he wanted to date her in the first place.

When the side door slammed shut behind him, he realised how easily he had been duped.

'Albert, get in quick!' Donna yelled. 'They're leaving!'

Shocked that there was a young man now trapped in the back of the van, Albert debated arguing, but Donna was right, the men he suspected of firebombing his bed last night were leaving and there was no time to lose.

As he got in, a panel between the cab and the cargo bay opened. It was smaller than a letterbox, but several fingers appeared through it followed by an angry eye.

'I can't believe you are kidnapping me,' snarled Toby.

His voice startled Rex, who wasn't expecting someone to speak right behind his ears. He spun around and barked. The noise, which was deafening in the confines of the van's cab, was followed a second later by the sound of Toby's body hitting the floor of the cargo bay.

'That ought to be keep him quiet,' muttered Donna, thinking the boy ought to be thankful she was including him. Then she remembered she still didn't know what the men from Blake's had bought. She leaned across to look through the gap. Toby was sitting, and looking very angry, on a sack of flour. 'What did the men buy in the wholesalers, Toby?'

His response was not printable.

Albert knew that people spoke like that, especially young people it seemed, but he did not approve. He was just about to admonish the young man when Donna replied with a tirade of expletives which ought to have set her mouth on fire. Albert wasn't even sure what some of the words meant.

When Toby didn't reply, opting for silence instead, Donna tried a more gentle approach. 'Albert and I are trying to help everyone, Toby. My shop and yours. Can you tell me what they bought? Please? It might be important.'

Albert thought the young man was going to remain tight-lipped, but he gave in, begrudgingly reeling off the list of items he'd seen on their cart. 'But that's almost exactly the same as you just bought, Donna,' he pointed out.

'Yes, it is,' she murmured in response. 'Why would two mechanics, fake or otherwise, be buying flour, lard, milk, eggs, and other ingredients. You can make a lot of things with it but buying it in those proportions indicates a serious intention to make a lot of something. Why would they even have an account at the wholesalers?'

'Maybe they are using someone else's.' suggested Toby, adding something useful for the first time.

'Can you do that?' asked Donna.

'Sure, if they know your face. I suggested dad just send the guys today, but he wouldn't have it. He wants a Simmons involved in every stage of everything we do.'

Donna added his points together. 'That would mean they weren't there for the first time then.'

Albert grimaced, annoyed with himself for missing a simple trick. 'It also means we should have asked whose name was on the card they used. That might have told us a lot.'

'Maybe we can circle back later when we find out where they are going,' suggested Donna.

It was a good idea, but for now, Albert was focussing all his effort on keeping up with the mechanics. He felt a bit more confident now that he had driven the van around a bit, but he was doing forty just to keep them in sight and it felt like warp speed.

Despite that, he didn't lose them, Toby sticking his head up against the hole again to see out of the windscreen.

'It won't be far now,' said Albert, dropping back so he wasn't always in their rear-view mirror.'

Mystified, Donna asked, 'Why do you say that?'

'Because we turned off the main road a while back and the streets are getting narrower. They'll pull into somewhere soon. Can you drive, Toby?'

'Of course,' Toby replied proudly.

Albert slowed the van to a stop. 'I'm getting out here. Toby can drive you back home.'

'Home?' Donna didn't understand.

'This was all about your business not failing, remember? You mum's staff are coming around this afternoon to start baking. It's the thing you need to concentrate on.'

Not exactly convinced, Donna asked, 'What are you going to do?'

'I'm going to walk Rex.' Rex's ears pricked up. 'I'm less visible by myself anyway. Nobody will notice an old man walking a dog. If I happen to see something I think might interest the police, I'll give them a call. There's something going on, that's for sure. You go bake some pies. I'll give you a call later.'

'If you're sure,' Donna said slowly. 'He was right that she needed to get baking. The future of her mum's shop might depend on it. Leaving Albert to snoop around after the criminals didn't seem like a good idea though.

Toby helped make up her mind. 'He said he's sure, Donna. Let him out and let's get out of here. Okay? I'll forgive you for shutting me in here and I'll take you home. If the crazy old man wants to play Hercule Poirot, then let him have at it.'

Donna wanted to drive home herself so she could do it erratically and throw Toby around a bit. Maybe that would knock some gumption into him. She'd never had a lesson though, so tempting though it was, it remained a fantasy.

Albert got out anyway, leaving the engine running as he held the door open for Rex Harrison. 'It'll be fine, Donna. Maybe they are just making pork pies,' he joked. 'They're in Melton Mowbray after all.'

Donna really wasn't happy about letting Albert go off by himself, but she couldn't do both things and she didn't want to let her mum down. Not only that, she recognised for the first time ever, what her mum had always said about wearing a business hat. Donna would inherit the pork pie shop and all the business that went with it. The trade had sustained her family for generations, keeping them afloat when things were lean and making a small fortune in better times.

In addition, she had a responsibility to her mum's staff; they needed jobs they could depend on, and she had a responsibility to herself to keep the business strong. All that meant she had to focus on getting pies made right now.

Toby drove not only quietly, but sedately, which surprised her. She watched him get behind the wheel anticipating a need to shout for him to slow down and take care. When he did speak, what he said surprised her. 'My dad prefers your pies, you know.' She looked at him in mute shock. Toby glanced her way, then smiled to himself and put his eyes back on the road. 'He'd kill me if he knew I told you, but he's spent his life moaning about how he cannot replicate your recipe. When he thought he got it close enough, he went into business. It's all he ever wanted to do, mum says. The pastry still isn't crisp enough and the filling just doesn't taste quite the same as yours and believe me when I tell you he has tried thousands of variations.'

She couldn't help but frown. 'Why are you telling me this?'

Toby didn't take his eyes off the road as he searched for words. He shrugged more than once and tried to make a sentence. In the end, he settled for, 'I didn't mean what I said. About your boobs, I mean. I think they are very nice.'

Pulling a face, Donna replied, 'You haven't seen them, Toby. How could you possibly know?'

'Fair point,' he conceded. Then with a cheeky grin and a glance at her chest, he said, 'I could judge and score them now for you, if you li ...' Her phone hit him just behind his left ear. 'Ow!'

'You mind your manners, Toby Simmons or you'll never get the chance.'

They lapsed into silence, their childish flirting reaching no conclusion as neither would admit they liked the other and both unsure what to do about it. All too soon, they were back at her house.

'I'll give you a hand in with the flour,' Toby offered as he shut off the engine.

'No need,' Donna replied. There were four members of her mum's staff waiting on the doorstep. They were a little early, but it meant they could get on straight away.

Jacob and Alan were quickly followed down the path by Mandy and Denise. Donna waved enthusiastically as she pushed her door open and dropped to the pavement. 'Thank you all for coming.'

They weren't looking at her or the goods inside the van when she opened the side door; their eyes were all on Toby Simmons as he rounded the truck to hand Donna back her keys.

'You're one of the Simmons bunch,' said Alan sternly, making his disapproval clear.

'Sleeping with the enemy,' commented Denise.

Donna's jaw dropped open. 'I am not sleeping with him!'

'It's a turn of phrase, Donna,' said Denise with a bored sigh. 'Come on team, let's get these goods inside and get to baking. Your mum will want to see deliveries going out when she gets back. I do hope you haven't been telling him your mum's recipe.' It was said as a joke because no one would ever reveal it.

Donna made a mock horrified face. 'Mum would kill me.' The team were already carrying the sacks, bags, and cartons into her house, using a key Donna handed Alan to gain entry. Toby loitered a few feet away, waiting to say goodbye. It had been an odd couple of days, Donna thought as she picked up the eggs with both hands and kicked the van's side door shut. Somehow, she seemed to be friends with Toby Simmons again despite almost pulling his scrotum off an hour ago.

'What are you going to do now?' she asked.

'I'll walk into town. The shop is only five minutes away. I guess I'll see you later?'

'Sure.'

Toby dithered nervously for a moment, then realised that was what he was doing, turned about with a reddening face, and hurried away.

Where Albert got out was right on the edge of an industrial estate. It was busy with cars, vans, and lorries going back and forth from the numerous units trading there. He saw plumbing supplies, a timber merchant, electrical wholesalers. Some of them were national franchises and others were independent family outfits. Not all the units were occupied but he could not find the van he followed into the estate. He looked through windows and went around the hundred or so units twice just to be sure. By the time he was ready to admit defeat, he was starting to sweat, and his back was getting sore.

He didn't know he was being watched.

'You say he followed you here?' Brenda asked.

Mikey had been driving so the question was aimed at him, but he wasn't sure how to answer. The old man had followed him, they spotted him inside the wholesalers and then again in their rear-view mirror but were not able to lose him on the way here. In the end, Mikey gave up trying to work out how Brenda might react and just admitted the truth. 'Yeah, he did.'

'That's quite remarkable seeing as how you killed him last night.' She took her eyes off the old man and his dog to glare at her two incompetent assistants. 'That was what you told me, wasn't it? "He's dead Brenda, we torched his room." He doesn't have so much as a sunburn!' she raged.

'So, we'll do it now,' said Malcolm, heading for the door. 'I'll snap his neck and then ...'

'No.' Brenda spoke with quiet insistence. 'It's broad daylight outside and there are people all around. He hasn't spotted us. That's the second time he's gone past. We need to clear the unit. Get everyone and everything out and be ready to torch it all. We'll do it tonight.'

'What about the old man and his dog?' asked Mikey, annoyed that his perfectly thrown firebomb hadn't hit the mark.

Brenda turned and walked away. 'He is insignificant. Do your jobs. We are clearing house and moving on.'

Outside, Albert accepted defeat. He'd already looked in too many windows and found someone looking back with a curious expression. Maybe they just circled around and left the area again. It was possible they spotted him following and brought him here to lose him. If that was the case, he'd helped immensely by getting out to go on foot.

Regardless, he couldn't find them, and it was time to move on. Maybe it was a fool's errand anyway. He left the trading estate, heading for the town centre, but a mile later discovered he was lost. Walking around aimlessly looking for something that wasn't there had got him all turned about so now he didn't know which way was which. He knew his phone had a compass on it and it had a map function, the young man in the store had shown him how to work it, but he couldn't make head nor tail of it now.

'I'll ask for directions,' he told Rex just to hear someone speak and wished there was a park so he could find a bench to sit on for a few minutes.

Inside the house, the team, including Donna, quickly fell into an assembly line routine. The longest serving was Denise, who started at sixteen straight from school in 1967. The newest member was Jacob and he had been with the team since before Donna was born. Theoretically, Donna was their boss, but she wasn't going to start throwing any weight around. They seemed happy to work as a team, so she asked what she could do to make the process slicker and did the jobs no one else wanted. They were the experts, after all.

Jacob kept eyeing her sideways and he looked a little nervous, glancing away every time she caught his eye. Telling herself it was her imagination, she carried on lining the pork pie dollies so the ladies could swiftly produce the pie base once the pastry had been given time to rest.

The air in the kitchen was thick with a soupy, meaty smell from the boiling bones and trotters. The herbs and vegetables in with them did little to mask the scent. On one counter, the men were carefully cutting the meat, taking their time and getting it right because that was one secret the Simmons missed.

It was a family tradition to hand cut the meat because it remained more tender that way. Using machines to slice it introduced too much bruising and failed to provide an even mix. Their way limited production, but the results were superior.

Donna had lost count of how many pork pies she had made and baked in her life, but it was a tiny fraction compared to Denise and Mandy who must be able to count off millions. Denise was firing handfuls of dough on their counter, stamping and shaping them with a dolly, then Mandy grabbed the raised pie base, expertly stuffed and pressed a softball sized pile of meat into it before slapping a lid on top. Then it got hand crimped and placed on a tray for baking.

It was fast. Too fast to believe. Certainly too fast for the cooking process which took forty-five minutes. When they ran out of trays to stack the uncooked ones on, Donna called time for a break and offered to make tea for everyone.

'Got any biscuits?' asked Alan, hopefully. 'I'm quite partial to a chocolate digestive, if you've got any going. A bourbon would do at a push.'

Donna pointed. 'Check the cupboard by the refrigerator.'

Jacob was still glancing nervously in her direction. She'd had about enough of it, but Denise prompted him to speak before Donna could. 'Go on, man. Just spit it out and get it over with.'

Donna's gaze flitted between Denise and Jacob. 'Spit what out?'

Jacob looked at the floor as his cheeks coloured and he began to fidget his hands now that he was on the spot. 'Um. Well …'

Donna thought she knew what this was about. It occurred to her when she saw the bloody mark on the skylight. The thumb fell through, but it couldn't have fallen onto the meat because it was in the refrigerators.

'Oh, for heaven's sake,' sighed Alan. 'Jacob found the thumb the other morning and rather than doing what he should have done, he put it on top of one of the class's piles of meat. There, Jacob, it's done now.'

Jacob had the decency to look wretched, but Donna was still stunned by the revelation. Her first reaction was to scream at him for all the damage and trouble he had done, but seeing how bad he looked, she stopped herself before the first word formed. Instead, she calmly asked,

'Why?' She'd guessed right; that someone had to have picked it up and added it to the meat, but she still couldn't believe it.

Jacob mumbled something no one heard.

Denise, always ready to boss them about said, 'Speak up,' raising her own voice to make a point.

'Belinda,' Jacob said, this time making himself heard.

Donna still didn't understand. 'What about Belinda?'

'She's an unpleasant, stuck-up, know-it-all, old cow,' Denise supplied.

Thinking to herself that she already knew that, Donna put two and two together. 'So you thought you would play a trick on her?'

Jacob nodded, finally bringing his eyes up to look at the teenager. 'I'm really sorry. I just didn't think it through. There was this thumb just lying on the counter. I know I should have done something about it, but I just didn't think. Belinda had been in bossing me about just a few minutes before, complaining that the meat portions weren't even enough the previous day which was an absolute lie. She always found something to moan about, so I gave her something worthwhile for once, sneaking into position the thumb on top of a pile of meat. Then when the police asked about it, I panicked and told them I had no idea how it got there.'

The timer on the oven pinged.

'That's the first batch done,' Mandy grabbed them out and set them on the side so the aspic could be added.

Denise eyed them critically. 'They want another two minutes. Your mum's range isn't setting the temperature accurately. I'll turn it up just a touch, but these ones need a bit longer.'

The pies looked perfect to Mandy, but she wasn't going to argue with half a century of experience.

Interest in the pies had broken the moment but Jacob was still looking at Donna as if expecting an answer. 'Am I fired?' he asked.

Everyone stopped talking to hear her response. Inside her head a small voice said, *'Wow. I really am the boss. They all think this man's livelihood is my decision.'*

'No, Jacob. Thank you for telling me the truth. I can contact the police now and maybe get the shop reopened a little quicker.' He tried to apologise again, but she waved him to silence as she picked up her phone, saying, 'Just don't do it again.'

Her comment drew a laugh from everyone except Jacob, though he did smile with relief that his secret was out, and the burden lifted.

Donna took herself out of the kitchen to make the call. She still had the card from DS Moss and got through to her straight away.

'Detective Sergeant Moss.'

'Hi, this is Donna Agnew from Agnew's Perfect Pork Pie Emporium. I know how the thumb got into the meat mix. One of the staff did it.'

There was a beat of silence before DS Moss spoke. 'I see. That's nice and convenient, don't you think?'

'What do you mean?' Donna hadn't expected disbelief as a reaction.

'You're desperate to reopen your business. You cannot be bothered to wait for police procedure so you have threatened or otherwise coerced one of your staff into claiming they did it so you can clear the matter up as quickly as possible.'

'No!'

'Young lady, you and that old man have caused me nothing but trouble since that thumb was found. I would like nothing more than to pretend I believe your story and sweep the whole thing under the carpet. One of us has to be an adult though.' Donna was getting really angry now, but she couldn't get a word in. 'Send your member of staff to the station to make a formal statement. If they dare. If I find they have given false testimony, I will make sure they are charged. Anything else?'

'No, nothing else, thank you.' Donna stabbed the red button to end the call, wished she had something to kick, and called Albert.

'Hello.' Albert answered the call. 'Is that you, Donna? How are the pork pies coming along?'

'All good. The first batch are out of the oven already. I called to let you know that it was one of the guys at the shop who put the thumb in the meat. He lied to the police but I'm going to send him to the station shortly so he can make a statement.'

'That's good news. It erodes some of the mystery.'

'Yeah. Do you need to carry on snooping now? The police did tell us to back off.'

Albert thought about it for a moment. There was no imperative to find out what the men from Blake's Auto Repair were up to. Not anymore. Mark Whitehouse would be found or he wouldn't but with the CCTV footage, the admission from a member of staff, and the hopefully soon conclusion of the forensic test to make sure the meat was pork and pork alone, the shop would be allowed to reopen and that would be that. The national drug squad would continue their case and he could go to Bakewell to make a tart and never think about it again.

The only problem with that scenario was that not knowing would keep him awake at night. It had made him a good detective many years ago: the inability to let things lie. Doggedly, he would pursue a case, picking at the edges until he solved it. He hadn't felt this alive in a long time. Certainly not since Petunia died a year ago.

'I think I'll just poke about a little more, since I am already here,' he told Donna. 'I'm sure Mrs Worsley would like to know why her house was firebombed.'

'Are you sure, Albert. You could just come back here. Mum doesn't get out of hospital until tomorrow. I have a houseful of freshly baked pork pies. You could sample them.'

Albert chuckled at how tempting that sounded. 'Tell you what, Donna. I'll start meandering my way back to you now. I'm a bit lost so it might take me a while, but if I can find it again, I want to swing into that wholesaler and ask them about the card the two mechanics used.'

'Shall I send someone to get you if you are lost?'

'If I could tell them where to find me, I wouldn't be lost,' he pointed out. 'Don't worry about me, Donna. The promise of a fresh pork pie will see me through.'

With the call ended, Donna couldn't shake the feeling that the old man was going to get himself into bother. The police were already upset with his interfering, but it was the likelihood of the criminals spotting him that worried her most. There was an organised crime gang behind whatever was going on at Blake's, that was what Albert said. It was drugs or something. It didn't really matter what it was, they were clearly serious people and tried to kill Albert because his dog sniffed around their place. They were capable of killing, and Albert was one little old man out there by himself. Well, okay, he was with a rather large and quite aggressive

143

dog, but still. A man lost his thumb and that was the only bit of him found so far. He was missing, as was another man from the same business - from a pork pie business.

The two men from Blake's had pork pie ingredients on their cart. Was that a link?

Several miles away, Albert was following the same line of thought. It was why he wanted to go to the wholesalers. A lady walking her poodle had been kind enough to give him directions back to the main road. He felt sure he could reorientate himself from there.

The thumb finding its way into the meat might have been a silly act by a member of Agnew's staff, but it became the catalyst for everything that happened afterward. To Albert, it felt like seeing the men from Blake's at the wholesalers today was an important clue, he just wasn't sure how to interpret it. One thing he was certain of, was that the police here hadn't seen the clue and were not following the same trail of breadcrumbs he was. That went double for the National Drug Squad.

His career taught him that coincidence is so rare one can ignore it. Pork pies were at the very root of this mystery, though he didn't yet know how.

Rex trundled along by his human's side. He was getting thirsty and they seemed to have skipped lunch, one thing his human never normally did. They had been walking for an hour now, which was fine by him; there were lots of things to smell and scents to follow. He was running on empty though, his ability to scent mark his new territory reduced to nothing which was why he needed a drink.

When they got out of the van, Rex thought they were going to do something interesting. He could smell the two men from yesterday, the ones in the dirty place that resulted in his bath. He had hoped to get to play with them again, but his human walked him past them twice without going in. Now they were heading back toward the town centre.

Their route wasn't a direct line, although it did follow the route Albert recognised from following the van. Essentially, he was retracing his steps, albeit that he was driving earlier, and getting closer to the town's High Street. His route would join it at the far end, down by the two pork pie shops. It also meant he was close to Blake's and when he saw a fire engine parked in front of it, his feet steered him toward the cruddy auto shop.

There didn't appear to be much activity as he approached. Whatever occurred was long over, but as he neared, he got to see the devastation. Blake's Auto Repairs had been burnt to the ground.

There was a cordon of sorts, but the firefighters were taking it down. 'What happened here?' Albert asked a firefighter as he approached the fire engine. Rex sniffed the air, sifting and sorting different scents to see what he could find.

The firefighter was taking down the barrier tape erected around traffic cones to keep people back. She turned around when someone spoke to find an old man with a large dog. She had a similar dog at home. 'There was a fire,' she replied with a smile, giving him an obvious answer. When he cocked an eyebrow at her, she chuckled and gave him a proper answer. 'We've been on it all night. There were acetylene tanks inside. One exploded but we couldn't be sure there weren't more inside, so we had to keep damping it down. We've been here since before midnight. The chief only called it safe an hour ago.'

'It's quite a mess.' Albert looked at the twisted remains of the building. Where the steel frame reached superheated conditions, it began to wilt, and what remained looked like a candle left out in the sun. The office was completely gone; he couldn't even see where it had been, and anything left inside was destroyed. If there had been evidence of anything illegal inside, it would be hard to find now.

'You don't have a car in there for repairs, do you?' asked the firefighter carefully.

Rex nudged her hand – he recognised someone who would make a fuss of him when he saw one.

Albert shook his head. 'Thankfully not.' This was efficient criminal behaviour and that meant organised crime. He doubted his appearance yesterday had spooked them enough to pack up and move. Criminals at that level were not given to nervousness, but it may have been a contributing factor – they had thrown a petrol bomb through his window after all. Either way, they were gone, folding their fake business and clearing house to remove any evidence the police might be able to sift through.

To Albert, it meant he had, in all likelihood, missed his chance to solve the why of Mark Whitehouse's disappearance. It didn't really matter, he told himself as he stared at the twisted building. The firefighter made a brief fuss of Rex but was already back at the engine packing gear away.

Regular Customers

Jacob agreed to go directly to the station; Donna felt it couldn't wait and thankfully no one presented an argument. The pies were getting baked and much of the prep work of dicing the meat and making the pastry was done – they could manage just fine without Jacob if his confession meant they might get the shop reopened sooner.

He was good enough to give Donna a lift to the wholesalers. They opened at five each morning to cater to businesses who wanted their produce fresh each day and closed at three each afternoon. She either got there soon or would have to wait until tomorrow.

Despite what she said to Albert, she couldn't deny her own desire to find out what was going on, and she also wanted to help him since he had done so much for her. Calling the wholesalers would not have worked; she had to be there in person to ask her questions.

'Hi, Mitch,' she greeted the man at the door checking people's store-cards. Mitch had been the security guard there ever since she could remember and was one of those kindly uncle figures who always gave her a lollipop when she came in as a little girl holding her mum's hand. The practice only stopped a couple of years ago, in fact.

'Hello, Donna. Where's your mum?'

'She had her appendix out,' Donna explained. 'She'll be back soon.'

'Did you forget to get something this morning? I'll let you in, but you'll have to be quick.'

Mitch's attention was drawn to the next customer coming through the door. The wholesalers closed in fifteen minutes, so they were moving fast and trying to show him their store-card while running by.

When he looked her way again, she said, 'Actually, I'm not here to shop. I hoped you might be able to tell me something about another customer.'

Mitch raised his right eyebrow. 'What do you want to know?' he asked carefully, hoping this wasn't a teenage crush thing where she wanted to know if someone was single or not.

'Two men were in here earlier today. They paid for their goods and left right around eleven o'clock and they bought plain flour and lard and I can give you a full list if it helps. I need to know who they were.'

'Why's that?' Mitch wasn't sure where this was going, but customer information wasn't something he felt he ought to be giving away.

Donna hadn't thought this through, she realised, because now she needed a reason to request the information and she didn't want to tell him the truth. Saying the first thing that came into her head, she told him, 'They clipped mum's van before they left the carpark and they were quite rude about it. They refused to give me their details, so I thought if I knew who they worked for I could go straight to their boss. Mum expects me to be able to stand on my own now.'

Well that changed things. Donna Agnew might not be a little girl anymore, but she was hardly a woman either. Mitch felt a naturally protective instinct for her having raised four girls of his own. 'Right, just give me a few minutes, Donna. When I close the doors, you and I will go and review the CCTV footage from the till area. You can point them out to me, and I will tell you which firm's card they used.'

Donna did a mental fist pump.

Half an hour later, when she spotted herself entering the store and walking under the camera, she was firstly horrified by how big her bum

149

looked in the jeans she had on and vowed to never wear them again. She forgot about it soon enough when she spotted the two men from Blake's.

'That's them!' she jabbed a finger at the screen.

'What? Mikey and Malcolm? You must be joking. They're regular customers.' Mitch was eyeing her suspiciously. 'What's this really about, Donna? You can't tell me you don't know them.'

Feeling her face turn red because Mitch was politely accusing her of lying, which she was, she had to ask, 'Why do you say that? Why would I know them?'

Mitch gave her a disbelieving face. 'Because they work across the road from you at the Simmons pork pie factory.'

The news hit her like a slap to the face. Toby had been bluffing her the whole time! The whole Simmons family had fooled her completely. Hold on, though. She knew they didn't work at the Simmons pie factory. Only yesterday they were at Blake's Auto Repair Shop.

'Do they have their own store-card?' she asked, curious as to why Mitch thought they worked for the Simmons family.

'No. Come to think of it, they always come in with Adam Dodd, the factory manager. He's been coming for years, of course, but these two fellas started appearing with him a few months ago.'

A few months ago. 'Exactly how long ago, Mitch? Is it about five months?'

Mitch's eyes rolled upwards as he searched his memory. 'Something like that, yeah.'

Donna was out of her seat and moving. She called, 'Thanks, Mitch,' over her shoulder as she ran out of his security control room. It led her back out to the shop floor where workers were restacking shelves and sweeping the floor. One of them buzzed her out of the main doors but now she was on foot and alone.

Mikey and Malcolm, as she now knew they were called, were using a Simmons store-card and coming to the wholesalers with the Simmons factory manager. That explained the purchase of pork pie ingredients but not why they were making them. Did they work nights at the pork pie factory? She didn't think the Simmons ran a night shift. How much were the Simmons involved? That was the real question.

She called Albert, holding her phone to her ear and expecting it to connect. When it went straight to voicemail, she tried again. The same result. Telling herself he was just in a dead spot, she put her phone away and vowed to try again shortly.

Arriving back at the wholesalers, Rex recognised where they were. This was where he saw the two dirty, smelly men earlier. They were fun but they weren't here now. It didn't look like anyone was here now.

Albert walked up to the doors. They were very clearly closed for the day which he failed to anticipate. He glanced at his watch: half past three.

Above his head was a sign displaying their opening hours. Had he known, he wouldn't have stopped for a rest and to let Rex run around at the park they passed. He might still have been too late, but either way he was flummoxed now.

Why did he bother to go to the wholesalers? He couldn't answer that question. There really wasn't any point to it. The criminals he believed to be involved had moved on, Donna was in her house baking a ton of pork pies, and her mum would be out of hospital in the morning. He felt a sense of disappointment; that was it more than anything. For a couple of days, the old thrill of the hunt had returned, and he felt invigorated by it. Now it was gone.

With the wholesalers shut, the last opportunity he had to learn anything worthwhile was denied him. Refusing to feel sad about it, he focused on the freshly baked pork pie waiting for him at Donna's house. His natural inclination was to decline her offer of a room for free for a second night, but he knew it was based on his personal pride and nothing else.

Huffing out a breath through his nose, Albert pushed all thoughts of criminals, missing thumbs, and arsonists from his mind and started walking back to Donna's house. 'Come along, Rex. Let's go and see what Donna's pork pies taste like.'

Rex licked his lips in response. Actually, he rolled his tongue around his muzzle to almost lick his eyeballs, but it meant the same thing: yum!

Donna wasn't at her house, though, and Albert didn't have a key. There was no reason for him to have one; it wasn't like their house was a B&B. He knocked again, for the fourth time with the same result as the first three. Why hadn't he tried calling her? When the question occurred to him, he fished out his phone and found it to be dead. In the excitement of last night, his phone hadn't got a full charge and he hadn't considered it until now. His charger was in his bag inside the house, so his phone was dead, and it was staying that way.

'I am not doing very well today,' Albert commented.

Rex looked up at his human but didn't comment.

His legs felt a little weary, so he sat on the raised doorstep for a while to think, and with no one else to bounce ideas off, he talked to Rex. 'What do you think is going on here, Rex?'

Rex stopped panting for a moment to stare at his human. 'Really? You're asking me. I've been telling you what this was about for two days: the thing they taught me to alert for. This would be easier if you could read my expressions.'

Albert watched the dog tilting his head but wasn't sure what to interpret from it. 'Adam Dodd,' he said out loud. 'That's the name of the Simmons' factory manager. He went missing at the same time as Mark Whitehouse. There must be something in that. If we could locate him, maybe we could find out why he went missing.' Albert pushed his lips out and wiggled them about a bit, an absent-minded habit that occurred whenever he was thinking deeply about a problem that perplexed him.

His brain insisted everything was linked.

Pushing himself back to his feet, he announced. 'I think it's time we visited Simmons pork pie shop again, Rex.' Rex bounced to his feet. His human truly was wise. They couldn't get to the pork pies here; Rex could smell them the other side of the door, so they would go somewhere else for them. Rex didn't care where they went if there was a pork pie at the end of the trail.

Albert's arm was almost being pulled off by his exuberant hound. 'Slow down, Rex. The shop will still be there.'

Except it wasn't. Well, it was there, but just like the wholesalers, it was closed. Albert glared at his watch again, which read three minutes after five. The person he saw moving behind the glass door as they approached had been turning the sign around from open to closed. Standing in front of it now and looking forlornly through the glass at today's unsold items, Albert and Rex got to watch the steel security shutter being pulled down.

Rex glared up at his human. He felt like barking his displeasure. 'We didn't stop for lunch and now there's no dinner. I can't be the only one getting hungry.'

He wasn't. Albert's stomach gurgled at him. 'You're right,' said Albert, interpreting Rex's expression correctly for once to the dog's complete surprise. 'I think we should get something to eat while I think about what our next move might be.'

Sitting down at the same table he chose twice before, the Land Lover pub menu oozed with just as many tempting delights as the previous times he perused it.

He needed to place his order at the bar, where he also selected a pint of lager. He was thirsty from his day which made the longer drink than usual sound enticing. He rarely drank pints now, his weak bladder wouldn't allow it, but perhaps he could risk it this once to obey his thirst. He got a half for Rex as well, along with a bowl the barmaid found.

Just as he was about to head back to his seat, he spotted a phone at the end of the bar. 'Is that for public use?' he asked.

The friendly barmaid smiled. 'Yes. There's no charge for paying customers unless you want to call overseas.'

'Just a local call. Do you have a phone book?' He thought it was a long shot, but he wanted to try to find Adam Dodd. Everyone had a mobile these days, even Albert had one upon his wife's insistence. But he found A. Dodd listed in the phone book with a number and an address. He was about to dial it on the old-style push-button phone, but hesitated. Maybe he ought to check in at home first.

Gary liked to fret, so Albert called his number from memory, cursing the invention of mobile phones because he hadn't bothered to memorise Donna's number.

The call was answered immediately as if Gary had his hand hovering over the phone. 'Dad? Are you alright? I've been calling you for hours. Where are you? I'm nearly there.'

Bombarded by a string of questions, Albert attempted to decipher them, but it was last three words that stuck in his head. 'Nearly where?'

'Melton Mowbray. I've got Selina and Randall in the car with me.'

'Whatever for?'

Gary didn't bother to hide his exasperation. 'Because you've been getting into trouble, dad. You had me contact an old friend up there, pulling some strings to get you information. Then you called Randall to get

155

him to do the same thing. Did you really not think it would get back to me when your bed and breakfast got firebombed last night?'

In truth, it hadn't occurred to him that anyone would hear about it. 'It's really not a big deal,' Albert tried to argue.

His daughter's voice cut him off. 'We're coming to get you dad. You are going to move in with me and Phil. I've got the biggest house and there are no stairs. We can convert one of the rooms into a bedroom for you. It's all worked out.'

'Move in with … I have a house of my own, thank you. Now I only called to check in so none of you would worry. I wish I hadn't bothered,' he snapped irritably.

'Just tell us where you are, dad,' she begged softly.

They all thought he wasn't able to look after himself. They were running up here to save him from his own incompetence. Well, incontinence pants might be in his future, but he wasn't decrepit yet and he was going to show them just how much life was left in the old dog.

'I shall not,' he replied. 'You're all police officers. Come and find me.' With that he put the phone down and dialled the number for Adam Dodd. When it got no answer, he swore quietly and kicked the brass bar rail in frustration.

One good thing came from his children; his waning motivation had been kicked to the kerb. He was ready to kick down doors – not that he would, he'd probably break a hip and that would be the end of his culinary adventure. Metaphorically though, the criminals had better watch out.

He downed his pint in one swift hit, glugging it until the glass was drained and wiping his face with the back of his hand as he gasped his relief. 'Another, please.' The barmaid had a startled look, and a plate of dinner in her hand.

'I'll bring the drink over. Unless you want to eat this at the bar?' she asked.

Albert almost said yes, but his unbridled determination to see this through couldn't escape the ache in his back, so he plopped back into his chair, poured the half pint he bought Rex into his bowl, and tucked into his plate of spam, egg, and chips. Ten minutes later, with two pints and a hearty dinner in his belly, Albert set off back to the Simmons' pork pie factory. Whatever was happening, that was where it was at.

Simple Instructions

Brenda was ranting again. Of all the idiots to get stuck with, she had these two morons to suffer. It was all because they were the boss's relatives. He didn't want them under his feet, so he palmed them off on her. Her years of loyalty deserved better.

'Are you sure you've got that clear in your heads?' she asked.

Mikey and Malcolm both nodded vigorously. 'Yes, Brenda,' they replied in unison.

Brenda didn't believe a word of it. 'Good. Repeat back to me what I just said.'

Neither spoke, hoping the other would do it, then both tried to speak at once and then both stopped to let the other speak.

Brenda slapped her face into her right palm and pointed with her left hand. 'You. You tell me.'

Her outstretched finger was unmistakably fixed on Mikey, so he started reciting her instructions. 'Get all the freshly cooked crystal meth from the warehouse and take it to the pork pie factory at seven o'clock.'

'But on the wayyyyyy!' Brenda screeched, wondering how the idiot could have already forgotten the most important stage.

'Yes, yes, sorry,' Mikey blushed. 'On the wayyyyyy, stop off at the lock up to collect Mr Dodd because he is going in the pork pie mix tonight.'

'Just like Mark the other night,' added Malcolm, helpfully.

'Then what?' Brenda prompted.

Mikey recited the next stage, 'Then we make Mr Dodd show us how to operate the machinery while threatening to put him in the mix.'

'Which he doesn't know we are going to do anyway,' added Malcolm, feeling more confident now.

Mikey nodded thanks to his accomplice. 'Yes, which he doesn't know we are going to do anyway, and we get ready to show off our ability to run the operation for when the boss arrives.' He finished and looked proud with himself.

Brenda waited. Then she waited some more. A trickle of sweat ran out of Malcolm's hairline as she squinted her angry eyes at him. 'No?' she questioned. 'No other slightly important parts in the operation tonight?'

Both men turned inwards to look at each other in bewilderment.

'You make sure the explosives are set!' Brenda screamed. 'Oh, my word! How did I end up babysitting you two dummies?' It was all getting to be too much; the stress making her irrationally angry. The boss was visiting tonight and no matter what she did, Mikey and Malcolm were going to make a mess of it which he would then say was her fault.

She had no choice other than to kill Mark Whitehouse. It was a minor problem they could easily have overcome until Adam Dodd lost his nerve when they forced him to put Mark into the pork pie mixer. The idiot ran away but he wasn't bright enough to hide where they couldn't find him, so as a result, he would go in the mix tonight. After that they would torch the whole place to cover their tracks. Two murders were two too many and the police would catch up eventually. Staying at least two steps ahead of the police was a policy that had kept her out of jail, for the last thirty-five years. One brief stint as a teenager was enough to make sure she didn't go back. It was supposed to ensure she didn't commit any further crimes but knickers to that, peddling drugs was much too lucrative.

However, if these two idiots didn't sharpen up, they would all get caught. She felt like banging her head against a wall. Or, better yet, banging their heads against a wall until there was nothing left of their stupid, ugly faces. Brenda remembered the good old days when cops could be bought, and no one cared that she distributed the weed she brought in from Europe. She was her own boss back then, answering to no one, but she strayed onto someone else's turf and now she was working for them whether she liked it or not. It wasn't like she could go to the police.

Malcolm and Mikey were still hovering a few feet from her, thinking they should probably get moving but neither doing so in case she started screaming again when they did. Malcolm thought she was hard to please. It wasn't their fault Mark chose to tear his own thumb off to escape. She disagreed and claimed their methods were too inventive. Malcolm believed there was an art to their trade. You couldn't just give someone a beating as Brenda expected, this wasn't the nineties; some finesse was required. He and Mikey had put real thought into how to stop Mark fighting back. He accepted they failed to anticipate Mark tearing off his own thumb to escape, but he didn't see what she was getting so upset about.

Realising they hadn't moved, Brenda put her balled fists on her hips. 'If you two idiots are still in this building in two minutes time, I will kill you myself and feed you to the pigs.' When they started running, bumping into each other in their haste to escape, she shouted a final order. 'If you see the old man and his dog again, grab them. They can go in the mix too!'

That Donna couldn't get hold of Albert was a worry, though she told herself not to worry because he might be a little deaf at his age and not be hearing it ring. Or maybe it just ran out of battery. Regardless, she couldn't raise him, which meant she was on her own for now.

Her suspicions regarding the Simmons family had gone full circle to bring her back to the point where she thought they were once again behind it all. Two criminals, Mikey and Malcolm, were in the employ of the Simmons. On top of that, they employed Mark Whitehouse straight from jail. The thumb finding its way into her mum's shop might have been a complete accident, but they were up to something and she was going to find out what. Mum would get out of hospital tomorrow morning and Donna planned to have kept the family business afloat and put their major competitor in jail by then.

All she had to do was watch the factory and work out what they were up to.

Unbeknownst to both Donna and Albert, they were standing just a few yards apart a few minutes after five. Albert, staring longingly at the pork pies through the front door was on the opposite side of the building to Donna. She'd found a shadowy spot between a wheelie bin and a wall from which she could watch the loading bay and doors to the Simmons factory through a chain-link fence. Her position was low down, but she had a good view into the yard area.

The staff were leaving, which she thought was a good thing; whatever the Simmons were up to, it had to be something they were doing outside of normal hours, she surmised. She got comfy and settled in for a long wait.

161

It was boring.

This was her first stakeout and she thought it would be exciting. It was anything but. The staff all left and the car park at the back of the Simmons shop emptied which left nothing to look at. After what she thought was an hour, she checked her phone to see what the time was but discovered only twelve minutes had passed. She put it away again quickly. There were messages from her friends, but she didn't start opening them, afraid the light would illuminate her cubby hole and give away her position if there was anyone else out there.

An annoyingly long time later, she spotted something. A flicker of light across the other side of the yard, in a dark spot much like hers. It was gone now, but focussing on that spot, she saw it again when it flashed on a few seconds later. It was Toby Simmons doing exactly what she told herself she shouldn't. He'd turned on his phone and the light from it lit up his face. She could see who it was from fifty yards away.

But what on Earth was he doing?

Donna was in Noggin Alley which ran between the Simmons shop and its factory and the Olde Shoe Shoppe which used to make shoes, her mother said, but now sold the same labels and brands as everywhere else. There was no through traffic because it had been closed off at the far end long ago. Too narrow for a car, the alley provided pedestrian access to the rear of the shoe shop but nothing else. It was why Donna picked it as a place from which to watch and why she knew she was in trouble when she heard footsteps approaching.

All the shops were shut; there was no good reason for anyone to be coming down here at all. They were getting closer, with confident strides, but something else too. It sounded like …

Rex poked his head into her cubby hole. 'Hello, human.' The young female jerked back when he stuck his head around the side of the wheelie bin. He had been able to smell her even over the delicious odours emanating from it, but she hadn't expected him – another example of how poorly constructed human noses were.

Donna grabbed Rex's head so he wouldn't try to lick her as she poked her head out. 'Albert!' she hissed to make the old man look down. He was looking through the fence opposite and hadn't noticed her as he scanned the Simmons' yard.

He turned around at the sound of his name being called. Oddly, there was no one there and it wasn't until the voice hissed, 'Down here,' that he cast his eyes down to find Donna tucked into a hole behind a wheelie bin.

'What are you doing in there?' he asked.

'Get down!'

'What?'

'Get down!'

'What?'

'Oh, for goodness sake.' Donna broke cover to grab the man's arm and tug him into the gap. Even standing up, they were far less visible tucked against the wall than he was right out in the open. 'I'm watching Toby Simmons,' she hissed.

Albert raised his eyebrows, following her finger to squint where she pointed. 'Where?'

'In that gap behind the generator,' she whispered.

'What's he doing?' Albert was keen to hear.

'Nothing,' Donna whispered in response.

Well that was boring news. Albert thought he ought to bring her up to speed on his investigation. 'I couldn't find the van this afternoon. I looked all over and managed to get myself lost, as you know. When I found myself again, I was near the Blake's place and the bookies where I got ripped off. Blake's yard was burned to the ground, nothing left.'

'Really?'

'It had a feel of finality about it and that tells me whatever they are up to is coming to an end. It might be that the police are getting too close, it might be something else, but whatever the reason, I think we either catch them at it tonight or they will be gone for good.'

'Oh! I went by the wholesalers earlier.' Donna remembered what she wanted to tell him.

'I went there too, but they were shut.'

'What time was that?'

'About half past three,' Albert replied, checking his memory to make sure he had it right.

'Oh. Yeah, they shut at three. Anyway, the two men we saw at Blake's and again at the wholesalers are called Mikey and Malcolm. I don't know their last names, but they were using the missing factory manager's store card.' Donna made a gasping face to show how big of a revelation she thought that was. 'And Mitch, that's the security guard there, he said they were in most days and had been for the last five months.'

Albert got what she was telling him. 'Ever since Mark Whitehouse got out of jail and got the job here.'

'Yeah. The Simmons family must be in on it. The whole dirty lot of them. I bet Toby's mum is behind it all.' Something occurred to her. 'Hold on. Why are you here? I came because I couldn't get hold of you, and the police lady, that cow, Detective Sergeant Moss, told me to get stuffed. Plus, I found out about the connection to their factory manager. Why are you here?'

'Because my kids want to put me in a home,' Albert growled. 'That, plus everything we have seen so far has been to do with pork pies. Your mum's shop isn't the connection, so it must be this place. With Blake's gone, if they are cleaning shop and moving on, then they'll be here tonight.'

'Shouldn't we call the cops. Oh, hey, I've been trying to call you for hours.'

'Phone's dead,' he replied, not taking his eyes off the spot Donna claimed to contain Toby. 'But, yes. We should call the police ... once we have something to tell them. DS Moss will want hard evidence that there is something going on before she will react this time.'

Donna nodded, squinting her own eyes as she tried to make out if Toby was still in the same spot. She hadn't seen him move for a while but couldn't find him anywhere else. 'Can you see, Toby?'

Albert shook his head. 'I think we should get closer. In fact, I think we should work our way around to him and find out what he is doing.'

'Won't that give the game away?' He'll know we are on to him.'

Albert drew in a slow breath through his nose, it was policeman's hunch time. 'I don't think the Simmons are involved at all.'

'What?' Donna asked, her voice dripping with disbelief. 'Their factory manager is the one going shopping with the criminals.'

Albert pointed a finger at the factory. 'Yes, and he has gone missing. A man get's out of jail, gets a job in a pork pie factory and sees an opportunity. Or he already had a contact here, Adam Dodd perhaps, and he came here because of an opportunity. Mark Whitehouse is a serial criminal. No one in their right mind would hire him to be security guard but I think we'll find out that Adam Dodd hired him. The Simmons family knew nothing about this until you tipped Toby off earlier today. He's over there doing exactly what you are doing over here: staking the place out and waiting for the bad men to show up. The fact that the factory manager was going to the wholesalers to buy goods rather than have them delivered here tells me he was up to no good. It's time to find out what that was.'

Donna didn't like it, but it made more sense than the family across the street being mixed up in something. Toby wasn't clever enough or brave enough to be a criminal. She nodded and stuck her head out from the wall to glance about. 'Okay, we'll have to go back to the High Street and work our way around unless you want to climb a wall.'

'I think the longer route might be more sensible.'

It took five minutes to go back up Noggin Alley, keeping low so Toby might not see them, and then going right around to come at the factory from the other side. There was a pedestrian entrance that side so staff coming in didn't have to walk in through the same gate as the heavy vans and lorries.

Donna led Albert on, taking his hand as they sidled along the far end of the factory. If Toby hadn't moved, they were about to swing around the corner and find him. Donna stopped at the edge, risked a very quick

166

glance around the corner and saw Toby sitting on his bum with his back against the generator. Having got bored waiting for something to happen, he was playing games on his phone.

Donna put a finger to her lips again, telling Albert and Rex to keep quiet, but unable to keep the smile from her face. Albert wondered what had amused her until she jumped out and shouted. 'Ha!'

Toby squealed like a little girl for the second time that day, dropped his phone, and tried to run away from the scary thing coming to get him. The result was that he cracked the screen on his phone, clonked his head against the unforgiving steel of the generator's outer casing, and wet himself a little bit.

Albert thought it amusing but unnecessary given the circumstances but followed Donna around the corner to find the boy sprawled on the floor with one hand on his chest and the other holding his head.

Donna was in a fit of giggles. 'I really got you that time,' she managed to get out between gasps of air.

'That wasn't funny,' Toby argued, just as breathlessly.

Feeling a need to be the adult, Albert kept a straight face. 'What are you doing, Toby? It looks like you are hiding.'

Toby scraped his legs around to get them back under his bum and rubbed his head where he hit it. 'I am hiding. Or, at least, I thought I was, but you two saw me I guess.'

'It's your phone,' Donna told him. 'It lights up your face like a Christmas tree. Why are you hiding?'

Grumpily putting his phone away, Toby clambered off the concrete. 'I got to thinking about Mark and Adam. I think there is something going on, but I don't know what it is. I checked the business account; mum doesn't know I know where she keeps the password. Anyway, Adam's store card for the wholesalers got used today right when we were there, and I think it might have been the two men you were following. Dad thinks I'm at football practice, but I skipped it for once. I'm no good anyway. I wanted to see if there was something going on here at night.'

Donna had to admit she had it wrong; he wasn't involved which probably meant none of his family were. She asked a question, 'What do you think might be going on?'

Toby shrugged. 'Maybe they are baking pork pies to sell on the black market and using our factory at night so they don't have to buy their own equipment.'

Albert raised an eyebrow, but Donna reacted first. 'Black market pork pies? Toby you are a plonker.'

Rex sniffed the air. Even outside the factory, it was thick with the smell of lard and pork. He wanted to eat something, but as he sifted the air and categorised the different scents, he detected the thing he was supposed to alert for again. It was faint, just like it had been the very first time he picked it up two days ago, but it was there.

'I need to visit the gentlemen's room,' announced Albert. The ill-advised two pints of lager had made his head swim a little, but the bigger impact was on his bladder which was now full and beginning to protest. Stakeout or not, he needed to find somewhere to relieve himself really soon.

Donna grimaced. 'There are public toilets at the other end of town. It's quite a walk.'

Toby fished out a bunch of keys. 'Use the toilets in the factory if you like.' He selected a key. 'This will open that door,' he pointed. 'Just lock up again when you come out.'

'Thank you, young man.' Albert took the keys gratefully.

'We should move,' said Donna, addressing Toby. 'You're too visible here. There's a better spot in Noggin Alley.' To Albert, she said, 'We'll be there when you come back out.'

Albert shuffled off to find the gents', taking Rex with him. Inside the factory, all was quiet. All the machines were off which made it eerily quiet, his footsteps echoing off the steel. Rex sniffed deeply once again, the smell of the drug he recognised just a little clearer now. There wasn't any here, at least, what his nose detected was no more than a tiny, trace amount, yet it had been here in the last few days.

Albert looked around, trying to remember if he had seen a sign for the toilets the last time he was here. Seeing no clues, he picked a direction and started walking. It took him back to the shop end of the factory where Toby's mum, Lisa, led the class in. Right next to the door was a sign with an arrow showing him which way to go for the restrooms.

It was restroom singular but that was all he needed. Rex circled the small room, feeling a little shut in when Albert closed the door with them both inside. There were lots of interesting smells, but his ears pricked up when he heard a vehicle stop close by.

Albert saw his dog react but thought nothing of it. Rex might have heard anything. It could be a mouse fart the dog just reacted to. He flushed and went to leave the toilet but then he heard it too:

Voices.

Rex pawed at the door to get it open. 'Stupid human's and their need for doors. Why are you always shutting things?' he whined at his human.

Albert put a steadying hand on the dog's head. 'Quiet now, Rex. I think we might be in trouble.' He opened the door just a crack so the voices might be easier to hear, then pressed his ear to the gap.

Rex shoved his nose through, taking a sniff and instantly getting a strong hit of the drug. He sucked in a breath to sound his alert but stopped when his human clamped a hand over his muzzle.

'Shhhh!' Albert whispered insistently. 'No barking, boy. Let's go see what is happening.' He couldn't hear what was being said, the noise was bouncing off the steel machines and echoing just like his footsteps had. Thinking that, he slipped his shoes off, his feet in socks making no noise at all. Albert cursed himself for letting his phone battery die; this had to be the criminals back here to do whatever it was they had been doing. It was enough to confidently call the police, but he didn't have the means to do so. There would be phones in the offices, if he could get to one.

Maybe Donna and Toby spotted them arriving and already called for help. That sounded likely. Then he heard something that chilled his blood.

'Don't touch me!' shouted Donna.

'What do you guys want,' wailed Toby.

They weren't calling for help. They had already been captured! Albert continued to sneak around the factory, checking around corners to make sure no one was there before he stepped out into each new walkway. He needed to get to the door and get out. He could find someone and raise the alarm if he could just find his way out again.

Suddenly, he recognised another voice. It was the awful woman from Blake's Auto Repair. 'Tie them up. Be quick about it,' she snapped.

Albert altered his route to get a closer look and Rex tugged at his lead; he wanted to go faster. He could smell that Donna was scared and he didn't like it. Something worried her and Rex could also smell the grimy men from yesterday and the woman they were with at the mechanic's place.

Donna and Toby protested and made it sound like they were trying to fight back. The unmistakeable sound of the round being chambered in an automatic pistol stilled them. 'Do that again, and I will shoot you.' Silence followed until the woman said, 'That's better. 'Now get Adam in here. Since you two idiots failed to learn anything in the last few months, he'll have to show you how to work the machines again.'

'Yes, Brenda.' Albert heard both men reply. They were going to collect Adam, which meant he was still alive, and they had him. That was why he went missing. Pondering the news meant he almost got caught listening as they made their way toward him. He only realised they were heading his direction at the last moment.

Adrenaline spiking, he ducked behind a large machine pulling Rex in tight next to him so they were out of sight just before Mikey and Malcolm strode by. He waited there, tucked in the dark until the men came past again. Peeking out, he saw them as they went by - they were carrying someone! It had to be Adam Dodd, the factory manager. He was wrapped in clingfilm and looked to be naked. His arms were flat to his sides and his legs were together like an Egyptian mummy.

As their footsteps faded, Albert slipped out of his hiding place to sneak a little closer.

'I'm not going to help you!' Albert heard the desperate fear in Adam's voice as he defied his captors.

Confidently, Brenda replied. 'Oh, I think you will.'

'No, I won't. You're just going to put me in the meat mixer like you did to Mark. I won't show you how to turn the machines on.'

Toby wailed, 'You put Mark in the meat!' His exclamation was followed by a clanging noise.

'Did he just faint?' asked Mikey.

Brenda walked up to Adam and lowered her gun. 'Why did you run away, Mr Dodd? Did you think we wouldn't find you?'

'Your goons put Mark in the meat mixer!' he blurted.

'Goons?' Mikey questioned, feeling the term was a little harsh.

'Shut up,' Brenda snapped at him. Then she pulled her trigger and shot off Adam's little toe. One moment it was there and the next it wasn't. Adam howled and fell to the ground, toppling like a felled tree since he could barely bend in his clingfilm wrapping. 'You have a lot more bits that I can shoot off yet, Adam. If you help me, I promise I won't put you in the meat mixer.'

'Yes, you will,' he cried.

Brenda bent down so she was close to his head then spoke to him in soothing tones. 'Adam, Mark's death was entirely his own fault. He demanded more money. You must realise that I cannot allow such behaviour. He hid that night's product and came to the repair shop to demand I pay him more.'

'You tore his thumb off!' Adam yelled through gritted teeth.

173

'Not true,' Brenda calmly replied. 'He did that to himself.' She glared at Malcolm and Mikey. 'My goons,' she used Adam's word, 'were supposed to give him a beating but they thought it might be easier if he was less able to fight back so they put his thumbs in two vices to hold him still. Remind me again what happened next, Malcolm.'

Head bowed, Malcolm sighed. 'Mark tore one of his hands free, leaving his thumb behind, hit me with a spanner, got free, and legged it.'

'Yes,' sneered Brenda. 'The point, Adam, is that I had to kill Mark. You don't have to join him though, if you do as I ask. We have plenty of meat tonight with our two volunteers. What's your name, volunteer number one?' Brenda sounded like a game show host introducing contestants to an audience.

When Donna's shaky voice answered, Albert knew he had to act quickly. He'd underestimated the criminals badly. Convinced they were involved in drugs, he allowed himself to be swept along by the excitement of the investigation. He knew how ruthless drug dealers were; Donna's predicament was his fault. It was time to get help here and he needed to do it quickly.

However, the moment he started back toward the door, he heard it open and yet more voices coming inside. His exit cut off; Albert darted away along a walkway running crossways to his.

A man's voice rang out. 'Brenda?'

Brenda knew he was coming but he was early. Too early. They weren't even nearly set up yet and she still needed to deliver the bad news that they had additional witnesses to dispose of. She raised her own voice to reply. 'Gregory. We are in the middle of the factory. I will send Malcolm to guide you in.' Then at a lower volume, she snarled. 'Get moving, you fat oaf.'

From his position tucked out of the way, Albert watched Malcolm jog by and then come back with three more men in tow. Two wore suits and looked dangerous. Between them was a much smaller man in a shiny new black tracksuit and box-fresh white running shoes. That had to be Gregory, and from the way other people acted around him, he had to be the man in charge. He looked about thirty, his dirt-brown hair cut short all over. His skin was as white as white, his features rounded and pudgy like a well-fed schoolboy. Albert only got a glance as he went by, but the stakes just got a lot higher: not only was the big boss here, but the amount of people to deal with just doubled.

That wasn't the worst part though. Just as Albert was about to edge his way back around the machinery to head for the door, the group led by Malcolm paused. Gregory said, 'Anton, wait by the door. This place makes me nervous. You know how I hate to leave my own turf. Make sure no one comes in or out.'

Albert glanced down at Rex. They were trapped.

Scuffle and Kerfuffle

Donna couldn't stop her knees from trembling. Adam, a man she recognised but didn't know, was bleeding onto the concrete floor of the factory. His little toe was missing. She wanted to feel sorry for him but was far too engrossed in worrying about her own future. Tied up and held at gunpoint, her little adventure had taken a terrible turn down Grisly Death Street. How on Earth was she going to get out of this? The ghastly woman from the repair place kept smiling at her – she was enjoying herself.

Albert was in here somewhere; she prayed he would be able to call the police, but as Malcolm came back into view with two men just behind him, she felt like she was running out of time to get rescued.

'Who's this?' A man in a tracksuit demanded to know as he jabbed a finger in her direction. Donna figured he must be Gregory.

'It's Nancy Drew,' Brenda chuckled. 'She's been snooping around, and she was rude to me. She can make a fine addition to the next batch of pork pies.' Donna felt like throwing up.

Gregory wasn't paying her any attention, nor was he focussed on what Brenda was saying. He was looking around. He arrived almost an hour early on purpose, planning to catch her out. Arriving on time, she would have things nicely organised to show him what she thought he wanted to see. Arriving early meant he got to see what she would be trying to hide. 'Why can I not hear the machinery running? You tell me that production has been forced to halt through unforeseen circumstances. Circumstances which necessitated my visit. A visit which you attempted to tell me wasn't necessary.' He brought his eyes to rest on Brenda. 'Do you feel you have this all under control?'

'It was a minor issue, Gregory, nothing more. The night watchman tried to blackmail me for more money and the factory manager,' she took a pace and kicked Adam, 'ran away when we put the night watchman in the meat mixer.'

'So why is he still alive?' Gregory wanted to know. 'Why are any of them still alive? You convinced me you had a perfect operation here.'

The cop part of Albert was loving all the information the criminals were divulging. If he were able to record it, convictions for all would be a cinch. Unfortunately, the rest of Albert was stuck in this room and things were getting desperate. He needed to save Donna and Toby for a start, plus Adam because he didn't believe Brenda's claim that she would let him live. To do that, he was going to have to risk his own life.

'The operation was perfect,' Brenda almost snapped. Getting talked down to by a man half her age was making her angry. 'I have shipped product all over the country hidden inside pork pies. Sniffer dogs cannot detect it, no one suspects it, and were it not for the greed of one stupid night watchman, you would be counting the proceeds and congratulating me on a job well done.'

A machine started up in a distant corner of the factory. They all heard it, Brenda, Gregory, and all the others exchanging glances. 'Who else do you have here?' Gregory demanded.

'No one,' she assured him. 'Where are your men?'

Gregory shouted, 'Anton?'

'Yes, boss?' His voice came from the other end of the factory, diagonally opposite where the machine noise still rumbled.

'Did you touch anything?' Gregory shouted.

177

'No, boss.'

Gregory cut his eyes at his second henchman. 'Go kill whoever that is, enough time has been wasted on talking.' The man needed no further instructions, jogging from the small area they were in with his gun drawn and ready. Once he was gone, Gregory turned back to Brenda. 'I shouldn't have to come here to ensure my business interests are represented correctly. This operation is a farce.'

Brenda's face became thunder. 'If you hadn't insisted I employ your idiot cousins, everything here would have been ten times slicker. They're to blame for the problems.'

'You dare to accuse my family? You are the one in charge, their failings are yours,' argued Gregory.

As they fell to bickering, only Donna thought she knew who caused the machine to come alive. She felt very alone, but a ray of hope crept in because that had to be Albert creating a distraction so the police could raid the building and save everyone.

A shot rang out, which made Donna flinch with its suddenness. 'That's how you do it,' said Gregory. 'All this putting people in pork pies is an unnecessary distraction. Shoot them, take the body away and move on.'

Brenda was getting really quite agitated. 'You know as well as I that any enterprise has a limited lifespan. We're going to make one last batch of porkpies using these three clowns ...'

'You said you'd let me live if I helped,' wailed Adam from his position on the floor.

'I changed my mind,' she roared. 'We'll work out how to run the machines ourselves. Dispose of the bodies, move the product, and then the place will be reduced to atoms. There are explosives in the van. The police have been sniffing around, but if we destroy all the evidence and move on, the trail will go cold. They're too dumb to work it out.'

'Oh, I wouldn't say that,' said Albert as he leaned casually against a machine. 'You must be Gregory,' he said to Gregory. 'If you are wondering where your man is, I'm afraid I had to kill him.'

'You? You killed Max? You look like you're a hundred and thirty years old.'

Albert chuckled at Gregory's insult. 'I'm afraid the game is up. Everything you've said since you walked in here has been recorded.' Albert turned to look at Brenda. 'We caught Brenda a while back, you see, and she cut us a deal. She is just a minnow after all. You're the big fish the police want.'

Gregory's eyes were as wide as saucers. He bought Albert's story hook, line, and sinker, spinning around to look at Brenda just as she raised her gun. She intended to shoot the old man, but Gregory misinterpreted her motion, thinking she was aiming for him, and shot her before she could get her gun lined up.

As the bullet struck her shoulder to spin her around, Albert said a phrase he hadn't imagined he would ever use. 'Sic 'em, boy!'

Rex came bounding around the corner with his teeth bared. Moving fast, his coat rose and fell and the muscles beneath his skin contracted and stretched. This was much better than chasing a man in a padded suit.

There were four targets that Rex could see: the two grimy men, the old lady, and a new guy in a tracksuit. Tracksuit man had a gun in his hand. Rex knew what it was and that it represented danger. It was pointed across the room in the general direction of the girl he liked. His back legs propelled him into the air on a collision course with his target. The man's face registered fear about a half second before Rex bit down on his right bicep. The gun went off, a loud noise that made Rex's ears ring, but it was followed quickly by a squeal of pain as Rex's bodyweight bore the man to the ground. Having immense fun, Rex shook his head a few times, tearing skin and tasting blood as the man screamed his surrender. The gun flew out of his hand to skid across the room.

In the meantime, Brenda, bleeding from the wound to her left shoulder, was getting up and she was mad as all hell now. Forget the product, forget money: this operation was ruined. Her new plan was to kill everyone and set up somewhere new by herself. She could hire her own people. First, though, she was going to kill the old man and the annoying, gobby girl. Lining up on the old man, she saw Gregory's gun skitter across the floor to stop right by the old man's toes. He was bending down to pick it up, but she was going to shoot him first.

Malcolm punched her in the head. 'Idiot, am I?' he bellowed. He had a new plan too. He was going to kill Brenda for being such a cow for the last five months and then he and Mikey were going to run away to some remote part of the country and get jobs in a pub.

While his fellow henchman dealt with Brenda, Mikey grabbed Donna. The witnesses all had to be disposed of and quickly so he and Malcolm could escape. Adam was wriggling like a worm in his plastic wrap shell, trying to get away but going nowhere, the boy was still out cold on the floor, so Donna was the one he needed to tackle first.

Rex spat out Gregory's arm, picked his next target and leapt for Malcolm.

Hearing the sudden commotion, Anton started running from the door. It meant he was leaving it unguarded but hearing Gregory shout in pain, he knew he was needed elsewhere.

Donna was caught in a bearhug, her hands tied behind her back so she could struggle, but escape was impossible. Mikey weighed at least twice as much and was at least twice as strong. 'I'll drop you in headfirst, love,' Mikey wheezed in her ear as he dragged her up a short flight of open-mesh stairs. 'You won't feel a thing that way.'

'No!' she bucked against him.

Mikey lifted a flap to reveal a button and turned the meat mixer/mincer on. It thrummed into life, the electronic motor driving the blades to speed in less than a second. 'Good thing I know how to make this one work, isn't it?' Mikey chuckled.

Rex, bit Malcolm's backside. The man was bent over to retrieve Brenda's gun when the dog got to him and it made too tempting a target to ignore. Malcolm roared in pain but got his hand on the gun. As Rex snapped his body back, driving his teeth deeper into Malcolm's soft, fleshy behind, the man lost his balance and toppled.

Mikey flopped Donna against the edge of the machine so he could get a better grip to tip her in. In that momentary respite, she got a foot against the machine and shoved backward. It pushed Mikey off balance but not by enough to make a difference. He grabbed her in another bearhug. 'Feetfirst it is then,' he snarled.

He lifted her off the floor again, intending to drop her straight in. Then Toby hit him. He hadn't needed to bluff fainting, that actually happened. But when he came to, everyone was arguing so he kept still and listened until he heard the old man talking. Then a shot went off and everything was happening at once. His hands were tied behind his back, but this was his family's factory and he knew there was a sharp bit of steel on a railing behind him. Toby cut his wrist getting the plastic cuff off his hands, but he got free while everyone else was fighting, and went after Donna.

Mikey's head snapped back from the blow, but then he smiled through his split lip. Mikey had been around a while and his life as a hoodlum and general all-round bad person, meant he was able to take a punch, especially from a teenage boy.

With a sneer, he said, 'Not bad, kid. But you'll need to hit me a lot harder than that.' Then, paying no attention to the boy because he could deal with him in a minute, Mikey lifted the girl up to the edge of the mixer/mincer.

Donna was screaming for all she was worth. Mikey had her from behind so she was facing the machine and putting everything she had into finding something she could brace her feet against. Three feet beneath her, a set of stainless-steel teeth were whizzing around like the mouth of a giant mechanical shark and all Mikey had to do was drop her.

Toby hadn't used the spanner the first time he hit Mikey. It was on a hook next to the machine because they used it to adjust the end play on the meat mixer. He'd grabbed it as he ran up the short flight of stairs but hadn't wanted to risk hitting Donna as she struggled. Out of options, and Donna still bucking against the man, he swung it anyway, the round end of the large tool striking the man on the crown of his skull. He dropped like a stone.

He also dropped Donna, who plunged toward the meat mixer.

Malcolm was squealing like a stuck pig as the dog yanked at his butt again. He just needed to get his arm around his body, and he could shoot the stupid mutt, but each time he lined his gun up, the dog yanked or twisted his head again and the shot went wild. Dragged a yard across the concrete the next time the dog threw its body sideways, Malcolm's head hit something solid. It was the railing for the stairs leading up to the meat mixer. He grabbed it to steady himself. Now he could take the shot.

Coming from the door, Anton ran full pelt to get to his boss. It sounded like a fight. There were shots, screams, and what sounded like a werewolf tearing people apart. He had no idea what he might find, but he didn't expect a geriatric old man to be standing over his boss and holding a gun.

The gun wasn't pointed at his boss which was the only thing that stopped Anton from shooting him instantly. It was aimed across the small clearing at a man having his butt attacked by a large dog. Reaching a decision, Anton felt certain the old man and the dog were on the wrong side of the equation - he would shoot them both and get his boss to safety.

Malcolm squeezed the trigger. His gun was lined up on the dog's skull. He was going to shoot it right between the eyes.

Albert didn't want to shoot the man on the floor. However, he really didn't want him to shoot Rex Harrison. Were he younger, he would tackle the man bodily. It wasn't an option, so he accepted his role and lined the fallen boss's gun on Malcolm's chest.

Rex felt the bullet part the fur on his skull as it passed harmlessly between his ears.

At that moment, Albert heard someone skid to a halt behind him and turned to see the other of Gregory's henchmen pointing his gun right at Albert's face. Albert had enough time to curse himself for forgetting about the man at the door before the shot sounded.

Anton pitched over to fall dead at Albert's feet. Malcolm's shot had killed him.

Malcolm swore and pulled the trigger again, but the gun just clicked: it was empty.

Albert said, 'That'll do, Rex.'

Rex heard him but was having way too much fun to obey.

Just beyond and above him, Albert saw Toby whack Mikey on the head with what looked like a spanner. It was pleasing to see, but Mikey then dropped Donna who fell directly into the machine with an ear-splitting scream.

Albert's heart stopped.

Raid

The sound of commands being shouted filled the air as Albert watched the teenage girl fall into the machine. In the depths of his brain, he knew the voices were those of police officers raiding the factory and that was great news. They were too late to save Donna; nothing could get to her in time.

Toby slapped his hand down on the big red emergency stop button. As designed to do, the blades went from hundreds of rpm to a dead stop in a fraction of a second. It was a safety feature fitted to all such machines. Toby couldn't stop her from falling, but his quick thinking meant her shoes hit the steel teeth and stopped there.

Donna couldn't believe it. The machine had shut off. Her heart rate was through the roof, she was terrified beyond the ability for rational thought, and she knew she was about to die. Then, a heartbeat before the wicked-looking steel teeth started ripping her apart, the machine stopped.

Toby's face appeared next to hers, a big beaming smile plastered across it. 'I shut the machine off. There's an emergency stop button,' he said brightly.

'And you couldn't press it sooner?' she growled. She was going to kick him in the trousers when she got free.

Standing on the steel blades, the top of the meat mixer only came up to just above her waist. Toby looped his arms around her and pulled her out and back onto the raised platform. From their position several feet above the ground, they could see armed cops in tactical gear swarming through the factory.

Albert knew they would be able to see him in a few seconds, their coordinated shouts were closing in. It was over, and he could breathe a sigh of relief that none of his team had been hurt. The gun was still in his hand; he'd forgotten about it until now. It would make the cops jumpy when they saw it, so he started to bend down to place it on the floor.

The blow to his left side caught him completely by surprise.

A shockwave of pain washed through him as he tumbled, knocked forward by a rising shoulder to his left kidney. It was Gregory, it couldn't be anyone else, but falling forward and out of control there wasn't a thing he could do about it. Donna and Toby saw it too, but they were too far away to stop it from happening.

A second later, the cops reached the open area by the meat mixer. Albert heard them sweep around the corner behind him just as Gregory vanished between two pieces of machinery.

'Get down!'

'Get on the ground!' The air filled with shouted orders aimed at him and Malcolm, plus Brenda, Donna, and anyone else still alive and moving. The priority for the police was to secure the area. Once any possible threat had been eliminated, they could work out who was who and separate the good guys from the bad.

'Drop the weapon!' The shout reminded Albert that he still held the gun. He never got to put it down, so it was in his hand. He released it now.

Rex was barking at the cops. Overly excited, he recognised the uniforms, but felt threatened as they converged on him. They were pointing their guns at him.

'Rex!' Albert barked.

Rex stopped barking. His human was on the floor. He should have noticed. Humans were a bit rubbish at taking care of themselves, he knew that, it was one of their traits that made them so likeable. The other humans, the ones in uniform, seemed nervous, so he sat and gave them a wag of his tail.

Five minutes later, the report came back that Gregory, the man they really wanted to capture had slipped beyond their hastily erected line.

Albert was sitting on a plastic chair that Terrance had liberated from an office. Adam, Malcolm, Brenda, and Mikey were all in custody and outside in the carpark being treated by paramedics. Their injuries were not life threatening, but Malcolm was unlikely to sit down for a month or more. The cops found Max too, who wasn't dead despite Albert's claim. Albert hoped they would send someone when he found an iron bar and a place to hide. His arms didn't have a lot of strength in them but iron bar versus skull works every time. Max squeezed off a shot as he fell, but it worked in his favour as Gregory assumed Max had shot whoever was there.

Albert absentmindedly stroked Rex's head as Terrance, the National Drug Squad cop, came to sit on the steps adjacent to him. They hadn't left the open area by the meat mixer, the chaps from the National Drug Squad wanted somewhere to work out what the heck had just happened, and this was where they picked.

Donna and Toby were standing just behind Albert chatting quietly between themselves. No one had asked them much yet. The flurry of activity that followed the cops' arrival hadn't allowed for questions other than whether they were hurt and if they needed anything.

Now, though, Terrance's weapon was holstered, and he wanted some answers.

Albert beat him to it. 'How did you find us?'

Terrance rubbed a hand across his face. 'My boss got a call from the Chief Constable of Leicestershire.' He paused to see if that would register on the old man's face. When he saw a wry smile tug the corner of Albert's mouth, he continued. 'It seems he is an old friend of your sons.'

'That still doesn't explain how you found me,' Albert pointed out. He suspected Gary would make a call when he hung up on him earlier, but Gary had no idea where he was either.

'There's a tracker on your phone,' Terrance explained. 'I think one of your children activated it a while ago.' Albert rolled his eyes. That was why his daughter wanted to help make sure his phone was set up correctly. None of his children trusted him. 'My boss is on his way here. We had to move fast when the call came in so there wasn't enough time for a coordinated response. However, it seems we weren't really needed. You took care of it by yourselves.'

'I'm sorry the boss got away,' Albert gave Terrance an apologetic look.

Terrance waved him to silence. 'It's okay. You found this place, something we haven't been able to do, and there's a hundred grand in crystal meth outside, plus a big bag of explosives. We even know the name of the boss now: Gregory. You've helped us immensely.'

A commotion coming from the entrance door end of the factory drew their attention. Albert recognised the voices: it was his children. All three were here, able to breeze past the cordon outside by showing their police warrant cards.

'Dad are you okay?' asked Gary when a cop in uniform led them to him. Gary's younger siblings both fussed as well, and Albert knew he should be grateful for it.

'I'm fine. Really, I am. I hurt my hip a little when I got knocked to the ground, but this trip has been good for me, just like I said it would be.'

'Okay,' said Selina. 'But you're coming home now, right?'

'Home?' Albert grinned at them all. 'I'm off to Bakewell. Adventure awaits.'

'You can't be serious, dad,' Gary complained.

Welcome News

Albert slept as well as could be expected that night. He was bone tired but each time his natural rhythms turned him onto his left side, he would awaken as the bruising in his hip reminded him what a privilege it was to grow old.

His children all found rooms at a local hotel, crashing there for the night with a threat to try to make him see sense again in the morning.

Rex slept well too, but then he always did. His doggy dreams were filled with action scenes that night as once again he got to chase bad humans and bite them.

In the morning, with the sun beating brightly against the drawn curtains, Albert forced himself from bed. He had been in Melton Mowbray, the home of the humble pork pie and stage one of his culinary tour of Great Britain, for three days and was yet to have so much as a crumb of the town's most famous dish. Today that was going to change.

Donna's mum was coming out of the hospital this morning, returning home to find her shop still closed. It would reopen soon enough, and the staff were on the road today distributing their pies to customers. They would be back at the house later today to make the next batch. Unfortunately for the Simmons, their business was most likely going to be wiped out. Their factory was at the centre of a drugs operation that saw crystal meth smuggled all over the country hidden inside pork pies baked at night in secret. The drug manufacturers were able to send the drugs anywhere they wanted without suspicion. The pork pies weren't for eating, they were nothing more than a clever coating with a container of drugs hidden inside. Delivered to numerous distributers, the pies were discarded as the drugs were recovered. The Simmons factory would be all over the papers and internet this morning but not for a good reason and there was no way to keep the lid on the story about Mark Whitehouse. He had gone through the meat mixer and no one could guarantee bits of him hadn't ended up in a pork pie sold from the front counter of the shop.

Adam would testify, Brenda and the others would all go to jail, but the Simmons were ruined regardless.

Albert found fresh clothes in his suitcase, and once dressed, he made his way downstairs to find tea. The house was quiet, which he assumed meant Donna was asleep still. He remembered his kids when they were teenagers and the fun he had trying to get them out of bed on a Saturday morning.

'Come on, Rex,' he said quietly. 'Let's go for a walk.' Having learned where the spare key was kept, Albert took it with him as he set off with his large German shepherd. Returning half an hour later, he found Gary's car parked outside the house and all three of his children inside waiting for him.

He greeted them with the love a father has for his children, but also with the determination that they would not sway him from his chosen course.

'You're really going to continue on to Bakewell?' asked Selina.

'Yes.' Albert replied, beginning to get annoyed answering the same question. 'From there I travel to Cumberland to make sausage and then to Arbroath to see how they make Arbroath smokies. It will be several months before I return home.'

Selina didn't look happy, but she nodded her head and said, 'Okay.'

'Okay?' Albert repeated suspiciously. They had been arguing for half an hour, and that followed weeks of arguing before he set off.

'Yes, dad,' Gary replied. 'Okay. We can't stop you, so we will join you.'

'Excuse me?' Albert wasn't sure he'd heard him correctly.

'Randall will go first. He's going to Bakewell with you. Then we'll see how things go.'

Albert wanted to argue, truthfully though, having his kids join him was the best gift he could think of.

A knock at the door interrupted their conversation before anyone else could speak. Donna, who was in the kitchen with them but keeping herself out of the way while the old people argued, hopped off her barstool and went to see who it was. She wasn't expecting anyone; the staff weren't coming until lunch and it was too early for the butcher to be making a delivery.

To her surprise, DS Moss was on the doorstep, her junior colleague DC Wright standing a pace behind as usual.

'Good morning,' said DS Moss, 'I have news for you. I thought I would deliver it in person.' Albert heard the police detective speak and came to join Donna at the door. Seeing him, DS Moss smiled. 'Seems I was wrong about you, Mr Smith. Congratulations are in order it would seem.'

Albert gave a small shrug. 'I was just trying to help a person in trouble.'

'Modest too. That's not what I came here for.' Fixing her eyes back on Donna Agnew, DS Moss delivered her news. 'The forensic inspection came back clear: there was nothing but pork in the meat we took from your shop. You can reopen as soon as you like.'

'What about the health inspection?' asked Donna, barely able to believe it was true.

'All taken care of,' DS Moss replied with a smile, already turning away. 'Someone had a word with someone, I guess.'

As the two police officers reached the pavement, a taxi pulled up in front of the house. Donna squealed with joy and leapt down from her front door. Her mum's face was looking out of the taxi's back window.

Epilogue: Thumb-in-the-meat Pork Pies

His train pulled out of the station, slowly building up speed as he started his journey from Melton Mowbray in Leicestershire, to Bakewell in Derbyshire. Albert had been savouring this moment for days, unwrapping the perfect pork pie slowly as if it were performing a striptease for his taste buds.

Then he let it sit on the table for a few moments as he basked in its glory. From his backpack he fetched a container with a chunk of vintage cheddar, a wholemeal roll, a jar of piccalilli, plus a napkin and flatware. When he took the items out, he knocked his wallet loose. It tumbled from the backpack where he kept it on the floor beneath the table.

It was a fiddle to retrieve, and his fingers at full stretch snagged a loose piece of paper poking from the top first. Once he had it all back on the table, he put the piece of paper back in but then saw what it was – the receipt from his bet at Grand's Turf Accountants. Smiling to himself, he ignored his desire to toss it in the trash and left it in his wallet. It would serve as a reminder of his time in Melton Mowbray.

Chuckling that the horse might have won - he hadn't checked - he went back to admiring his pork pie.

'Are you ever going to eat that?' asked Randall.

'My boy, you fail to fully understand the majesty you behold. I, Albert Smith, hand-raised this porkpie myself. I rolled out the pastry, formed it with a dolly, put the meat inside it, covered it, baked it and added aspic fresh from the saucepan. This will be the best pork pie I have ever eaten, and I need to pay homage to the event.'

Albert got a raised eyebrow in response.

Rex was getting impatient too. He knew Donna's mum gave Albert an extra porkpie just for him to eat and his human was still to hand it over.

Randall's brow creased. 'What's with the pastry thumb on top?'

His children hadn't come with him to the shop so had missed all the excitement. Donna's mum called the staff to redirect them there. They were opening straight away and would have a special class for one as soon as they could fire up the oven. Then she called the local papers, including the one that hack Peterson worked for.

The town knew the story of the thumb in the pie and she made a sensation out of it, Denise and Mandy forming hundreds of pastry thumbs, so each pie now had one baked on top.

Donna placed a call to Toby and got the Simmons family to come to the shop. Donna's mum hired Lisa to replace Belinda, Toby and his dad were given jobs in the shop and the uncle was sent to work in the back with Jacob and Alan. No more would their rivalry negatively impact each other's trade. The Simmons' name was ruined but their shop would be converted along with their factory so Agnew's pies could be produced in greater quantities. The meat mixer/mincer would go, replaced by a team of people to hand-cut the meat and they would diversify to supply sausages and other associated treats.

Albert watched it all happen with a wry smile and a happy heart.

The Simmons hadn't known anything about Adam's extra-curricular activities. Toby's dad commented that Adam had always seemed tired but never once questioned whether he was working half the night as well as during the day. Adam ran the factory and did the hiring and firing of staff, supply of ingredients and supervision of maintenance. It was how he managed to hire a man directly from jail and, foolishly, Mr Simmons never once performed any kind of check.

To celebrate their reopening, Mrs Agnew went out into the street with all her staff, including the new hires, and gave away samples of their new thumb-in-the-meat pork pies. It was a huge hit, attracting a National TV station crew and making it onto the evening news.

Albert chose to slip away while they were being filmed. His elder son and daughter had already left for home and Randall was waiting for him.

Rex chuffing his impatience brought Albert back to the present and the very tasty-looking pork pie. As if about to perform a very delicate operation, Albert selected his knife, said a prayer, and cut himself a generous slice.

Rex licked his lips and whined. A snort of laughter escaped Albert's lips, but he unwrapped the second pie and gave it to the dog in six pieces, each devoured with equal ferocity and none having time to register on the dog's palate.

Then, without further ado, Albert picked up his slice.

The End

Except it isn't. There's a whole load more on the next few pages.

What happens next?

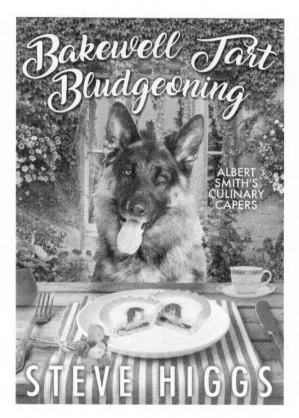

On a culinary tour of the British Isles, retired Detective Superintendent Albert Smith and snarky former police dog Rex Harrison find something quite unexpected waiting for them at their B&B

…

… it's the almost-dead body of their landlady.

Refusing to believe in coincidence, Albert and Rex set out to discover why her 'accident' is the second terrible event there in two days. Something is stirring in Bakewell and it's not the ingredients for a famous tart.

In trouble faster than a souffle can fall, the duo must work fast before anyone else has an accident. But the landlady's twin sister is hiding a secret, Albert keeps calling it a tart when it's a pudding, and their taxi driver, Asim, appears to use a language all of his own.

With Rex's nose working overtime, you can be sure they'll track down the bad guys responsible. Unfortunately, that might be when the real trouble begins.

Baking. It can get a guy killed.

Author Note:

Hello there,

Thank you for reading this far and for having enjoyed the book enough to wish to read the authors musings at the end.

I first conceived the concept of a man and his dog solving mysteries so long ago that I do not remember what year it was. The idea came from an article in National Geographic which I read some twenty-five or more years ago. It was about a man whose dog was injured and rendered quadriplegic. Unwilling to put the dog to sleep, he bought a Winnebago and toured North America, taking the dog in a harness of his design, to all the places he could think of to go. Their journey lasted months before the dog's condition deteriorated and he died while his human held him, and the sun set over the Rocky Mountains. I may have romanticised some of the tale, it was a long time ago when I read it, but the idea stuck.

Albert and Rex will tour the British Isles, soaking up the scenery and getting into various scrapes as they grow old disgracefully. I totted up my book ideas before I started writing this one and came out with seventeen without having to really think. I don't know how long the series might be when I finally retire the characters, or how well it will be received, but I shall enjoy writing it, regardless.

I am sat quietly in the log cabin at the bottom of my garden watching a breeze scare the blossom from my trees. It is a sunny day though still too cool to spend much time outside. It is set to warm up in the next few days which will thrill my four-year-old who is desperate to be in the new inflatable paddling pool we bought him.

By the time this book is published, the enormous watermelon my wife has hidden under her top, will have burst and we will have a daughter. It has been a long time coming but with the event almost upon us, I feel calm and ready. If I had to pick one dominant emotion, it would be impatience. I am impatient to hold my daughter.

I'll close this note now and let you get to whatever your next book is. It need not be one of mine; there are so many great authors out there. I have a Patricia Fisher story to edit and then another one to start writing, but I will be back with Albert very soon. The very observant among you might have picked up that Albert lives in the same village as Patricia and appeared, very briefly, in one of her books already. I wonder where that might lead?

Take care

Steve Higgs

PS. Don't miss the recipe and history of the dish on the next page.

Recipe and History of the Dish

A pork pie is a traditional British meat pie, usually served at room temperature. It consists of a filling of roughly chopped pork and pork fat, surrounded by a layer of jellied pork stock in a hot water crust pastry. It is normally eaten as a snack or with a salad. Personally, I eat them like an apple and at the time of writing, I will be visiting a farmers' market in nearby West Malling – readers of the Patricia Fisher series will recognise the name - where I will be able to find a selection of them.

Modern pork pies are a direct descendant of the raised meat pies of medieval cuisine, which used a dense hot water crust pastry as a simple means of preserving the filling. In France the same recipes gave rise to the modern Pâté en croute. Many medieval meat pie recipes were sweetened, often with fruit, and were meant to be eaten cold: the crust was discarded rather than being eaten.

The Melton Mowbray pork pie is named after Melton Mowbray, a town in Leicestershire. While it is sometimes claimed that Melton Mowbray pies became popular among fox hunters in the area in the late eighteenth century, it has also been stated that the association of the pork pie trade with Melton originated around 1831 as a side-line in a small baker and confectioners' shop in the town, owned by Edward Adcock. Within the next decade, other bakers then started supplying them, notably Enoch Evans, a former grocer, who seems to have been particularly responsible for establishing the industry on a large scale. Whether true or not, the association with hunting provided valuable publicity, although one local hunting columnist writing in 1872 stated that it was extremely unlikely that "our aristocratic visitors carry lumps of pie with them on horseback".

The main distinctive feature of a Melton Mowbray porkpie is that it is made with a hand-formed crust. The uncured meat of a Melton Mowbray pie is grey in colour when cooked; the meat is chopped, rather than minced. As the pies are baked free-standing, the sides bow outwards, rather than being vertical as with mould-baked pies.

In the light of the premium price of the Melton Mowbray pie, the Melton Mowbray Pork Pie Association applied for protection under European Protected designation of origin laws as a result of the increasing production of Melton Mowbray-style pies by large commercial companies in factories far from Melton Mowbray, and recipes that deviated from the original uncured pork form. Protection was granted on 4 April 2008, with the result that only pies made within a designated zone around Melton (made within a 10.8 square mile (28 square kilometre) zone around the town), and using the traditional recipe including uncured pork, are allowed to carry the Melton Mowbray name on their packaging

There is a tradition in the East Midlands of eating pork pies for breakfast at Christmas. While its origin is unclear, the association of pork pies with Christmas dates back to at least the mid-19th century and it was by far the busiest time of year for the Melton manufacturers. I remember my mother eating pork pie for breakfast at Christmas in the 70s and 80s. I thought it personal peculiarity until I studied the subject.

Being something of a carnivore, I have made my own pilgrimage to Ye Olde Pork Pie Shoppe in Melton Mowbray's town centre. I didn't get to raise my own hand-formed pork pie, though; it remains on my bucket list, but my loving wife has presented me, on several occasions, with a surprise box of goods from the shop which always includes a large pork pie and a selection of bite sized pies plus bacon, sausages, chutneys and more.

If you are one of those wonderful people signed up to my newsletter, you will have seen the pictures and comments when I bought my own dolly and tried to make this wonderful delicacy at home.

Ingredients

For the pastry

- 150g/7oz lard
- 50ml/2fl oz milk
- 50ml/2fl oz water
- 450g/1lb plain flour, plus extra for dusting
- salt and freshly ground black pepper
- 1 free-range egg, beaten, for brushing

For the pork jelly

- 900g/2lb pork bones
- 2 pig's trotters
- 2 large carrots, chopped
- 1 onion, peeled, chopped
- 2 sticks celery, chopped
- 1 bouquet garni (bay, thyme, parsley; tied together with string)
- ½ tbsp black peppercorns

For the pie filling

- 400g/14oz shoulder of pork, finely chopped
- 55g/2oz pork belly, skin removed, minced
- 55g/2oz lean bacon, finely chopped
- ½ tsp ground allspice
- ½ tsp freshly grated nutmeg
- salt and freshly ground black pepper

To serve

- piccalilli or chutney

Method

1. For the pastry, place the lard, milk and water into a small pan and gently heat until the lard has melted.

2. Sift the flour into a large bowl. Season with salt and freshly ground black pepper and mix well.

3. Make a well in the flour and pour in the warm lard mixture. Mix well to combine, until the mixture comes together to form a dough. Knead for a few minutes, then form into a ball and set aside.

4. For the pork jelly, place all the pork jelly ingredients into a large pan and pour in enough water to just cover. Bring slowly to the boil, then reduce the heat to a simmer. Cook for three hours over a low heat, skimming off any scum that rises to the surface, then strain the stock through a fine sieve and discard the solids.

5. Pour the sieved stock into a clean pan and simmer over a medium heat until the liquid has reduced to approximately 500ml/1 pint.

6. For the pie filling, place all the pie filling ingredients into a large bowl and mix well with your hands. Season with salt and freshly ground black pepper.

7. Preheat the oven to 180C/350F/Gas 4.

8. Line a pork pie dolly (or a jam jar) with cling film to prevent the pastry from sticking.

9. Pinch off a quarter of the pastry and set aside. On a floured work surface, roll out the remaining three-quarters of pastry into a round disc about 3cm/1¼in thick. Place the pie dolly into the middle of the pastry circle and draw the edges of the pastry up around the sides of the dolly to create the pie casing. Carefully remove the dolly from the pastry once your pie casing is formed.

10. Roll the pork pie filling into a ball and carefully place into the bottom of the pastry case.

11. Roll out the remaining piece of pastry into a circle large enough to cover the pastry case as a lid.

12.   Brush the top inner parts of the pastry casing with some of the beaten egg and place the pastry circle on top. Pinch the edges of the pastry to seal the pie. Brush the top of the pie with the rest of the beaten egg, then bake in the oven for 45 minutes to one hour, or until the pie is golden-brown all over.

13.   Remove the pie from the oven and set aside to cool. Cut two small holes in the top of the pork pie and pour in the pork jelly mixture (you may need to heat it through gently to loosen the mixture for pouring). Chill in the fridge until the jelly is set.

14.   To serve, cut the pie into slices and serve with piccalilli or chutney.

Recipe Tips

The pastry is best made the day before and kept in the fridge wrapped in cling film. Bring to room temperature before rolling out.

Final note: In Cockney Rhyming slang, pork pie rhymes with lie, so a familiar saying in England is, 'You're telling me pork pies.'

On a culinary tour of the British Isles, retired Detective
Superintendent Albert Smith and snarky former police dog Rex
Harrison find something quite unexpected waiting for them at their B&B
…

… it's the almost-dead body of their landlady.

Refusing to believe in coincidence, Albert and Rex set out to discover
why her 'accident' is the second terrible event there in two days.
Something is stirring in Bakewell and it's not the ingredients for a
famous tart.

In trouble faster than a souffle can fall, the duo must work fast before anyone else has an accident. But the landlady's twin sister is hiding a secret, Albert keeps calling it a tart when it's a pudding, and their taxi driver, Asim, appears to use a language all of his own.

With Rex's nose working overtime, you can be sure they'll track down the bad guys responsible. Unfortunately, that might be when the real trouble begins.

Baking. It can get a guy killed.

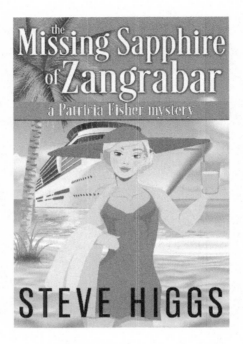

Read the book that started it all.

A thirty-year-old priceless jewel theft and a man that really has been stabbed in the back. Can a 52-year-old, slightly plump housewife unravel the mystery in time to save herself from jail?

When housewife, Patricia, catches her husband in bed with her best friend, her reaction isn't to rant and yell. Instead, she calmly empties the bank accounts and boards the first cruise ship in nearby Southampton.

There she meets the unfairly handsome captain and her appointed butler for the trip – that's what you get when the only room available is a royal suite! But with most of the money gone and sleeping off a gin-fuelled pity party for one, she wakes to find herself accused of murder; she was seen leaving the bar with the victim and her purse is in his cabin.

Certain that all she did last night was fall into bed, a race against time begins as she tries to work out what happened and clear her name. But the deputy captain, the man responsible for safety and security onboard, has confined her to her cabin and has no interest in her version of events. Worse yet, as she begins to dig into the dead man's past, she uncovers a secret - there's a giant stolen sapphire somewhere and people are prepared to kill to get their hands on it.

With only a Jamaican butler faking an English accent and a pretty gym instructor to help, she must piece together the clues and do it fast. Or when she gets off the ship in St Kitts, she'll be in cuffs!

What Sam Knew

Patricia Fisher is not your average woman. To start with she lives in a seventy-three-room manor house and travels with a Jamaican butler who is part ninja and fakes his Downton Abbey accent. Then add to those facts that she just opened a private investigations business and throw in the worrying bit where people keep trying to kill her.

When a climber suspiciously falls to his death and a local artist has her dog stolen, Patricia finds herself investigating two cases which seem to have no motive and no clues. Even with the help of her friends these mysteries will be hard to unravel.

But as she starts to poke her nose in where it is most definitely not wanted, a name from the past comes back to haunt her, a mysterious underworld figure issues a confusing threat and she begins to wonder if she has any idea what she is doing. Will her intuition get her through again? Or has she bitten off more than she can chew?

If only she had listened to Sam.

Get ready for a new series of thrills!

Free Books and More

Get sneak peaks, exclusive giveaways, behind the scenes content, and more. Plus, you'll be notified of Fan Pricing events when they occur and get exclusive offers from other authors because all UF writers are automatically friends.

Not only that, but you'll receive an exclusive FREE story staring Otto and Zachary and two free stories from the author's Blue Moon Investigations series.

Yes, please! Sign me up for lots of FREE stuff and bargains!

Want to follow me and keep up with what I am doing?

Facebook

Made in the USA
Las Vegas, NV
24 March 2024